Megan Peel

instruments othe...
was forced to take...
forgetting to bring...
moved to the Yorksh... ...usband,
...wo cats she fished out of a dustbin while on
...oliday in Greece, and a huge fluffy white dog
...it looks suspiciously like a Trumpenhund.
W... Megan is not writing, she enjoys gardening
...stilettos and feeding badgers sugar puffs.
...J ...other life, she would love to work for the
secret service. This is her first book.

Hannah Shaw is probably the m...
...u... ...usical person in the world and is a...le...
all ...usical instruments (especially phartleh...
...ie is, however, quite good at drawing an...
...v... ...ting. Hannah has illustrated lots of picture
an... ...hapter books for children, and some of them
ha... won awards – *Evil Weasel*, *Crocodiles Are the
Best Animals of All* and *The Great Hamster Massacre*.
When Hannah isn't drawing or throwing paint
around, she likes walking in the Cotswolds and
doing dog agility with her long-legged hound, Ren.

The Fabulous Phartlehorn Affair

Megan Peel

illustrated by Hannah Shaw

**WALKER
BOOKS**

This is a work of fiction. Names, characters, places and incidents are either the product of the author's imagination or, if real, are used fictitiously. All statements, activities, stunts, descriptions, information and material of any other kind contained herein are included for entertainment purposes only and should not be relied on for accuracy or replicated, as they may result in injury.

First published 2012 by Walker Books Ltd
87 Vauxhall Walk, London SE11 5HJ

2 4 6 8 10 9 7 5 3 1

Text © 2012 Megan Peel
Illustrations © 2012 Hannah Shaw
"Ain't No Mountain High Enough" by Nickolas Ashford
and Valerie Simpson © 1967 reproduced by permission of
Jobete Music Co. Inc./EMI Music

The right of Megan Peel and Hannah Shaw to be identified as
author and illustrator respectively of this work has been asserted by them
in accordance with the Copyright, Designs and Patents Act 1988

This book has been typeset in StempelSchneidler and Hannah Shaw font

Printed and bound in Great Britain
by Clays Ltd, St Ives plc

British Library Cataloguing in Publication Data:
a catalogue record for this book is available from the British Library

ISBN 978-1-4063-3180-6

www.walker.co.uk

In memory of my grandparents,
Audrey, Edward, Barbara and Trevor,
and also for Kit and for my godson, George
M.P.

"...ed elli avea del cul
fatto trombetta."
("...and he used his bottom
as a trumpet.")

Dante's *Divine Comedy*

A Windy Morning

A cold wind rattled through the streets of London. It ruffled the feathers of pigeons and whipped against the faces of all the busy people rushing off to work. Litter scuttled along the pavements and the trees tossed their branches, whispering and creaking as they swayed from side to side. Meanwhile, down in the tiny bedroom of a houseboat moored on Camden Lock, a very different kind of wind was blowing. Bruno Pockley woke up with a start and smelt trouble.

Sure enough, before Bruno could reach out and slam the cabin door, his grandfather's parrot swooped into the room.

"Pop goes the stinker!
Pop goes the stinker!"
squawked Chippy, landing on a
shelf above Bruno's bunk.

A second later, Grandpa Trevor came clattering
down from the deck to see what all the fuss was
about. Bruno watched as his grandfather's muddy
boots descended through the trap door, swiftly
followed by his skinny chicken legs and enormous
pot belly. Grandpa Trevor was a short man, and yet
once inside the boat, even he had to stoop to avoid
bashing his bald head against the ceiling. Not that
Grandpa Trevor would ever admit to being bald of
course. He was immensely proud
of the three silver hairs he kept
slicked across his forehead.

"Chippy!" the old man
scolded. "Leave the poor boy
alone. Bit of morning wind's just
nature's alarm clock. Isn't that
right, Bruno, love?"

Chippy flapped her blue and
yellow wings. She shrieked and
squawked and screeched. Then
she made the *briiinnng!* of an

8

alarm clock, followed by a loud squelching sound. Grandpa Trevor couldn't help but laugh. And when he did, his belly wobbled like a heap of frogspawn. Now he clutched at his stomach as if worried it might fall off.

Bruno slid back under his duvet and groaned. His curly brown hair stuck up from beneath the covers like a dirty mop. When would Grandpa Trevor understand that his unusual musical talent was not a laughing matter, but a very serious business? "Prodigious", that was how his parents had described it when they were around. *Prodigious*. Bruno liked the sound of that word. He didn't know exactly what it meant, but it had a very important ring to it.

Little did Bruno realize that very soon his prodigious parps would get him into more trouble than he could possibly imagine. For before the week was out, Bruno's extraordinary explosions would send shockwaves across Europe, spark an international manhunt and bring down the monarchy of an ancient Alpine kingdom.

But all that was in the future. Blissfully unaware of the dangers that lay ahead, Bruno Pockley rolled out of bed and padded off to brush his teeth.

2

The Boy with an Extraordinary Gift

The bathroom was cold and dank. A single
porthole looked out across the muddy brown
canal. Mould grew on the pipes behind the toilet,
and icicles hung down from the shower, dripping
freezing water onto the floor. And yet the damp
and, if truth be told, really rather smelly bathroom
was still Bruno's favourite place aboard *The Jolly
Codger*. For it was only here that he could practise
his parping in peace.

It didn't matter how much Chippy squawked or
Grandpa Trevor laughed. Bruno knew he was a boy
with a very special gift. Other people had to wait
to be surprised by a trump. Bruno Pockley was able

to produce them at will. He didn't need to stuff himself full of onions or garlic, cabbage or baked beans. Oh no, all Bruno had to do was to bend forward and suck in his stomach muscles until he felt a stream of cold air rush up into his tummy. Then, breathing out hard through his nose, he relaxed everything and gave a sudden shrug of his shoulders. BOOM! The air came hurtling out again like water from a whale's spout. And not only had Bruno taught himself how to trumpet on demand, he had also begun to learn how to control the pitch, length and volume of his parps. He experimented now with a three-note scale…

"Doh, ray, me," squawked Chippy from outside the bathroom. Grandpa Trevor tapped on the door.

"Come on, son, time to get dressed. Can't have you missing the school trip. It's all right for some, eh, Chippy? Lucky Bruno's off to spend a week at the seaside."

"Thar she blows!" screeched Chippy. "Thar she blows!"

Peels of Grandpa Trevor's laughter reverberated around the boat. Inside the bathroom, Bruno's heart sank. He'd been trying not to think about the dreaded school trip to France.

The only thing that Bruno hated more than being mocked by a parrot was his new school. Or, to be precise, his fellow schoolmates. The worst thing about St Ermingarda's School for Exemplary Young People was definitely the other pupils. Selfish and spoilt, the lot of them. And now, thanks to the dreaded school trip, Bruno was about to spend a whole week in their company!

The second worst thing about St Ermingarda's was the uniform. In Bruno's opinion, forcing children to wear shorts every day was clearly an act of child abuse, and should be illegal. It wasn't so much the cold Bruno objected to. It was how stupid he felt trudging off to school each morning in his grey shorts, purple blazer, long red socks and straw hat with matching red ribbon.

"You don't look stupid. You look smart." That's what Grandpa Trevor always said, proudly patting his beloved grandson on the back.

Fat chance of that, thought Bruno, as back in the bedroom he reluctantly changed out of his pyjamas. Smart was not a look he could ever seem to pull off. Maybe it was his lopsided grin or his slightly sticky-out ears. Or perhaps it was because one of his eyebrows was just a bit bushier than the other. Whatever it was, there was simply something untidy about Bruno Pockley's face. And no school uniform in the world could disguise it.

Tugging his tie into a tangled knot, Bruno opened the bedroom door and made his way into the smoke-filled kitchen. Grandpa Trevor was bending over the stove, frying up a pack of bacon.

"My, my, if it isn't little lord smarty-pants!" he exclaimed, cracking an egg into the sizzling pan. "Or should I say little lord *farty*-pants, eh, Chippy?"

The old man hooted with laughter at his own joke. He slapped his thighs. He wheezed and giggled and sniggered and snorted. Soon Grandpa Trevor was laughing so hard he had dislodged his comb-over. Bruno decided not to tell his grandpa that his three precious hairs were now dangling down from his head like a one-sided beard. Let him be the butt of the joke for once.

Still chuckling to himself, Grandpa Trevor dished up breakfast. As always, Chippy joined them at the rickety wooden table, perching on

13

the back of a chair while she gobbled down a plate of tinned pineapple chunks.

"Right," said Grandpa Trevor, shovelling in a last mouthful of toast and rising to his feet, "time to get this show on the road."

Like an ancient rock star signalling for his band to start up, the old man clicked his fingers and Chippy swooped onto his shoulder. Curious, she pecked at the dangling curtain of hair.

"Please, Grandpa," said Bruno, "does the parrot really have to come out with us? It's *soooo* embarrassing."

"Embarrassing?" exclaimed Grandpa Trevor. "Tosh! Who cares what other people think? I can't leave Chippy here. Think how lonely she'd be. Now off you go and put your shoes on. We'll be up in a second with your suitcase."

3

The Worst Day of Bruno Pockley's Life

Perhaps I should pause now to explain how an ordinary boy like Bruno ended up at an exclusive establishment such as St Ermingarda's School for Exemplary Young People.

To be honest with you, it's a very sad story. Sensitive readers should probably skip ahead to the next chapter.

Still with us? OK, so here's what happened.

For the first nine years of his life, Bruno did not live aboard a houseboat moored at Camden Lock with Chippy and Grandpa Trevor. No, he lived with his parents, Ronald and Jane Pockley, in a basement flat just around the corner. In general they were a very happy family, but sometimes Bruno's mother would get sad. She was the kind of romantic woman who would have liked to sit each night and watch the sunset from her balcony. Unfortunately the basement flat did not have a balcony. In fact it only had one window. To make matters worse, this window was at the back of a kitchen cupboard. There were bars across it to keep the burglars out.

"It's them who should be in prison, not us," said Mrs Pockley with a sigh.

Who'd want to steal muesli anyway? thought Bruno.

On summer evenings, Mr and Mrs Pockley would sneak up onto the roof of the flats to watch the sunset. Going out on the roof was strictly forbidden to children. So while Mr and Mrs Pockley were upstairs enjoying the view, Grandpa Trevor would come round to watch telly with Bruno.

One warm night in August, a year before our story starts, the grey clouds were just turning to candy-floss pink when a freak gust of wind caught the edge of Mrs Pockley's dress. She let out a loud squeal as her skirt billowed over her head like a huge cotton balloon.

Mr Pockley was
so distracted by this
unexpected display of
his wife's underwear
that he failed to notice
her feet had left the
floor. By the time he did,
Mrs Pockley's amazing skirt
balloon had already lifted her
half a metre above her husband's
head. All Mr Pockley could do was
to jump up and catch hold of her feet.
Soon the two of them were floating, up,
up and away towards the horizon.

Downstairs in the flat, Bruno heard the shrieks
of startled passers-by. He and Grandpa Trevor
rushed outside. A small crowd had gathered on
the pavement. Everyone was craning their neck

towards the sky. Bruno peered up in the direction of their pointing fingers. Could that be his parents floating far above his head? It was! He was sure it was.

Helpless, he watched as the silhouette of his parents got smaller and smaller. Soon they were just a tiny black speck against the sun.

Ten minutes later, the owner of the flats, Maximillian King, screeched up in a yellow Porsche. He was a high-flying businessman whose business it was to buy up the tall buildings in the city. You could tell just by the look of him that his life had been lived inside offices. His hair was as grey as a filing cabinet. His skin was as white as photocopyier paper.

"All blame lies with the deceased," announced Maximillian King as he came towards Bruno with a legal-looking document. "Now if the dependant will just sign here…"

Bruno was in such a state of shock, that without thinking he began to sign.

"Hang on a minute!" cried Grandpa Trevor. He snatched the pen from his grandson's hand. "We know our rights, and we're not signing anything!"

18

Maximillian King looked shocked. He was not used to being disobeyed.

"Very well," he hissed. "If that's the way you want to play it, I shall call my lawyer."

"For goodness' sake," shouted Grandpa Trevor, "the boy's parents have just floated off into the sky! He's not after money. What he needs right now is a hug."

This statement triggered a most peculiar reaction in Maximillian King. Despite being one of the world's richest men, the businessman had not been cuddled in more than twenty years. Much to everyone's surprise, he stepped forward and threw his arms around Bruno. His bottom lip began to quiver, and soon he was wailing like an orphaned kitten.

"Oh, my poor, poor boy. You're all lost and lonely like me," he whimpered. "Don't worry, Uncle Max will give you anything you want."

Bruno pushed him away in disgust. "All I want is my parents back," he said quietly.

Grandpa Trevor put his arm around his grandson and led him back inside.

An hour later a courier arrived with a letter. Grandpa Trevor read it aloud to Bruno.

Dear Mr Pockley,

Whilst I admit no responsibility in relation to the case of the unlawful levitation of your son and daughter-in-law, I would like to make a contribution to the education of the dependant. I have therefore taken the liberty of enrolling Bruno Pockley at my old Alma Mater, St Ermingarda's School for Exemplary Young People, and will cover all associated expenses.

Yours sincerely,
Maximillian King

"What does that gobbledegook mean?" asked Bruno.

"It means that you're going to a new school," explained Grandpa Trevor. "And Mr King's paying."

"But I like the school I'm at now," protested Bruno. "All my friends are there."

"The offer of an expensive education is too good to refuse," said his grandfather. "I've made up my mind. If you're going to come and live with me and Chippy on board *The Jolly Codger*, I'm not having you tread water at some second-rate school. Besides, it's what your parents would have wanted."

There was nothing Bruno could say to argue with that.

20

And that is the sad story of how an ordinary boy like Bruno ended up at St Ermingarda's School for Exemplary Young People. Where Mr and Mrs Pockley eventually came to land remained a mystery, but at least Bruno could console himself with the thought that his mother had finally achieved her dream of sailing off into the sunset with his father.

4

Nobody Important

On the day our story begins, Bruno had been at St Ermingarda's for just under a year. Every morning, whether the sky was dark with clouds or decked with sunshine, the somewhat reduced Pockley family would set off down the towpath and on through the vast green expanse of Regent's Park. What a peculiar sight they made: the old man with the parrot perched on his shoulder; the young boy traipsing along beside him in that old-fashioned school uniform. Bruno hated the way people would turn their heads to stare, barely able to hide their sniggers.

Today, the grass was still bubble-wrapped with last night's rain. Bruno's compulsory brown leather sandals squelched on the wet turf. Mud spattered the backs of his bare legs and his red wool socks felt soggy between his toes. If only he was still at his old school, where you were allowed to wear trainers.

"Come along, love," said Grandpa Trevor, turning to wait for his grandson to catch up. "No shilly-shallying. We'll never get there at this rate."

Walking at a brisker pace, it took them less than fifteen minutes to reach St Ermingarda's towering iron gates. As always, a pack of photographers crowded the pavement outside the school. No sooner had the photographers glimpsed Bruno's purple blazer than their camera bulbs began to flash. Chippy gave a squawk of indignation. Grandpa Trevor shielded his eyes from the lights.

"Hold it! Hold it!" shouted a photographer as they drew nearer. "Don't waste your batteries. It's nobody important, just that scruffy little kid from the boat."

As abruptly as it had begun, the flashing and clicking of camera bulbs stopped. *Nobody important.* The words rang in Bruno's ears as a security guard ushered them in through the gates.

"No one important?" scoffed Grandpa Trevor. "Who do those idiots think they're talking about?

One day you'll be more famous than everyone
else at this school put together! I can feel it in my
bones."

Bruno felt a flush of guilt. There was nothing
he wanted more than to make his grandpa proud.
But the old man had such high hopes of him. How
would Bruno ever live up to them? He wasn't the
cleverest in his class, nor the sportiest, nor the
most musical, nor even the best looking. Perhaps
the photographers were right. Perhaps he was
nobody important. That was what his classmates
thought, after all.

His classmates. Bruno could see them all
now, assembled on the gravel driveway with
their enormous designer suitcases, their parents
hovering over them like flies around manure.
At the edge of the crowd lurked the boy Bruno
disliked most of all. Humbert Maldewicks.
A talented violinist who bore an uncanny
resemblance to the young emperor Nero, Humbert
had a love of all things classical and cruel. The
gold ring that he wore on his little finger bore the
Maldewicks family motto: *If in doubticus, fibicus.*
Not a day passed in which Humbert was not
faithful to these words.

Bruno watched as Humbert disentangled himself from Mrs Maldewicks' embrace. It was hard not to laugh at the sight of Humbert's pale triangular face, pockmarked with his mother's lipstick like a bad case of acne. Humbert glanced up just in time to catch Bruno giggling. He scowled. Then a nasty smirk began to play about the corners of his lips. He brought two fingers together into the shape of a gun and pointed

them at Chippy. *Boom!* Humbert mimed blasting the parrot into the sky.

"*Emergency! Emergency!*" declared Chippy, flapping her wings in fright.

"That's my boy!" roared Mr Maldewicks and slapped Humbert so hard on the back he almost knocked him over. "Keep up that kind of aim and I'll take you with me next time I go shooting lions in the Serengeti."

"Really?" gasped Humbert, who couldn't think of a more exciting way to spend his summer holidays. "That'd be awesome."

"There you are, Bruno!" a voice called across the lawn.

Bruno turned to see Miss Goodwin heading towards them with a frazzled smile on her face and a clipboard in her hands. As teachers go, Bruno had to admit that Miss Goodwin was actually quite nice. In fact, she was one of the things that Bruno disliked *least* about St Ermingarda's. Most adults who spend their lives surrounded by spoilt children become as sour as shrivelled lemons. With Miss Goodwin, however, a deep well of natural kindness had helped her to remain as sweet as a peach. Even when she was trying to be stern, her blue eyes smiled softly under her long blonde fringe.

"Late again," she scolded merrily. "I shall have to put *you* in detention soon, Mr Pockley. It's your job to get your grandson here on time, you know."

"Who's a naughty boy?" squawked Chippy from beneath Grandpa Trevor's dislodged comb-over.

"Better late than never, eh?" The old man chuckled. "Anyway, a detention wouldn't be so bad if you were monitoring it, Miss Goodwin."

Bruno stared down at the ground in

embarrassment. Perhaps, on second thoughts, he should have warned Grandpa Trevor that his hair had come unstuck. Now the teacher was looking at him as if he was some kind of lunatic.

"I'm afraid," she said with a bemused smile, "that the time has come to say your goodbyes. Here, let me take that suitcase for you, Bruno."

Trevor Pockley bent down to give his grandson a hug. Bruno breathed in the familiar scent of warm jumper encrusted with fried egg.

"Mind how you go, love," said Grandpa Trevor. "Don't be sailing into any hot water. I'll be worrying about you, y'know."

Miss Goodwin put a reassuring hand on the old man's arm. "There's absolutely no need to worry, Mr Pockley. Your grandson can't possibly get into any trouble while he's with me."

And of course the kind-hearted teacher believed every word she said.

5

All Aboard the St Ermingarda's School Jet

For most people, a school trip means a few hours aboard a smelly old bus followed by an afternoon trooping around an ancient monument or museum, pausing every now and again to take a brass rubbing or to eat a sweaty packed lunch. Not so for the pupils of St Ermingarda's. For, as by now I am sure you've guessed, the pupils of St Ermingarda's were not most people. They were the sons and daughters of megastars and millionaires. They did not eat packed lunches or take brass rubbings and they most certainly did not travel by school bus. As far as they were concerned, there was only one way to travel – and that was by private jet. And not just any old private jet, either: a big shiny silver one emblazoned with the St Ermingarda's school crest.

The school grounds were easily big enough to accommodate a runway (between the many playing fields, heated swimming pools and tennis courts). Last year, before Bruno had joined the school, his class had flown all the way to Australia to learn to scuba-dive on the Great Barrier Reef. This year, as part of a project they'd been doing on the history of cinema, they were off to a film festival in the South of France.

"Blimey," Grandpa Trevor had said when he signed the permission form. "Best school trip I ever went on was to a hosepipe-manufacturing factory. Surprisingly interesting it was, too, watching how they got the holes in the rubber tubing. But a film festival – well, we didn't go on trips like that in my day. You make the most of this opportunity, my love."

"Yes, Grandpa," said Bruno, not wanting to sound ungrateful.

Just how ungrateful the average St Ermingarda's student was would have been obvious to anyone looking in on Bruno's classmates as they waited on the runway for take-off. Had you been there, for instance, stowed away beneath a seat, I'm sure you'd have been shocked to see the rows of children staring goggle-eyed at mobile phones and laptops. Only one girl was looking out of the window with excited anticipation of the journey ahead. This girl had bobbed brown hair, bright green eyes and a neat button nose. It was the first time she had ever been on an aeroplane. Her name was Grace Chalk and she was even newer to St Ermingarda's than Bruno. She had joined just a few weeks ago, at the start of the spring term.

On Grace's first day the headmistress had introduced her in assembly. "Please give a big round of applause to Grace Chalk, winner of our annual scholarship for exceptionally talented linguists."

Back at home, Bruno had looked up the word "linguist" in the dictionary. Perhaps this could be his special talent too. After all, if he didn't know what a word meant, how was he supposed to know if he was any good at it?

linguist/ *n.* someone with a gift for speaking foreign languages.

Bruno's heart sank. He was bottom of the class in French and German, and the only kind of Mandarin he would ever get his tongue around was the kind with pips and an orange skin. Here was yet another talent he did not possess.

The funny thing was that for someone who was supposed to be so good at speaking foreign languages, Grace did not seem very fond of talking. Bruno had hardly heard her utter a word since the day she'd arrived. She rarely spoke in class and she spent all her break times alone in the library. No doubt she thought she was far too clever to mix with anyone else.

The seat next to Grace was the last empty one on the plane. Bruno had no choice but to sit down beside her. Grace did not say hello. Instead she flashed him a brief half-smile before turning back towards the window. Oh well, thought Bruno, it's better than getting stuck next to Humbert for two hours.

"Sixty seconds till take-off," announced the pilot. "Please fasten your seatbelts and hand in all electronic devices."

Loud sighs went round the plane, followed by a bleeping chorus of mobile phones and laptops being switched off. Miss Goodwin collected them all up in a basket, to be handed back at the end of the trip. The pilot revved up the engine. Bruno clung tight to his seat as the plane sped off down the tarmac then climbed steeply into the sky. He peered over Grace's shoulder to see the grey expanse of rooftops give way to emerald swatches of field. Then the plane was wrapped in a duvet of cloud. Bruno's heart pounded in his chest. *Boom, boom, boom,* it went, like a timpani drum.

Perhaps you are wondering if Bruno was scared. Let me assure you that this was not the case. As befits the hero of our story, Bruno was a brave boy, as unafraid of flying as he was of rollercoasters or spiders. The truth was that a tiny part of him hoped to glimpse his parents floating past the window.

"Stop the plane!" he would yell. "That's my mum and dad out there!"

A much larger part of Bruno knew that this was a ridiculous idea. His parents must have fallen to earth many months ago. By now their bodies would be lying in some distant desert or at the bottom of a lonely ocean. Tears welled in Bruno's eyes as he imagined their bones stripped clean of flesh by vultures or piranh—

Splat!

Just as Bruno's daydream was becoming too terrible to bear, he felt something cold and wet land on his neck. Then whatever it was began to ooze slowly down his shirt. Bruno reached under his collar then brought his fingers back out again. They were covered in a glistening black slime and there was a reek of fish in the air.

"Eewk!" he said, wiping his hands on his shorts. "What's *that*?" Grace turned from the window. Her hand fluttered up to her mouth like a startled bird.

"Oh no," she whispered. "I'm so sorry. It's all my fault."

"Why are *you* sorry?" asked a bewildered Bruno, still trying to wipe the disgusting black gunk off his fingers. "It wasn't you, was it?"

Grace looked hurt. "Of course not," she protested, glancing nervously over her shoulder. "It was Humbert. That black stuff's caviar. Otherwise known as stinky fish eggs. Humbert often has it in his lunch box. He's found out that I'm allergic to fish, and now he thinks it's funny to throw food at me. Tuna sandwiches, smoked salmon bagels, pickled herrings – you name it. This time he must have missed and got you instead."

Bruno peered down the plane. Two rows behind them, Humbert sat smirking like a shark. Sure enough, there in his hand was an open tin of caviar. Raising the tin in a mock "cheers", Humbert slurped up a spoonful of the fishy black slime. Bruno unbuckled his belt and knelt up in his seat.

"You're sick in the head, you know that, Humbert?" he shouted. "Only a total coward would pick on someone about their allergy. How would you like it if I put a wasp's nest in your locker? Or stuffed stinging nettles down your pants?"

The children seated around Humbert began to titter.

Hearing the commotion, Miss Goodwin came rushing down the plane.

"Bruno!" she cried. "Wearing a seatbelt is for your own protection. If you need the toilet, just press the button and I'll escort you up the aisle."

Bruno slid back down into his seat, cringing with embarrassment. "Sorry, miss," he said quickly. "I was just, erm, stretching, that's all."

Miss Goodwin shook her head and returned to

the front of the plane. As soon as she was out of earshot, Bruno turned to Grace.

"You should've told her Humbert's picking on you," he said.

Grace folded her arms across her chest. "It'd just make things worse. Anyway, it's not like *you* told her Humbert was throwing stuff at you, is it?"

Before Bruno could think of a reply, there was an outbreak of singing from the back of the plane.

"Stink Bomb! Stink Bomb!
Bruno Stink Bomb!
He could take down Humbert
If he blasts him with his bum!"

Bruno didn't need to turn round to recognize the high-pitched wail of Xanadu Messiah Brown. Xanadu: the boy with a song for every occasion. Beneath his straw hat Xanadu wore a pair of silver reflective sunglasses that hovered above his nose like a pair of flying saucers coming in to land. The adopted son of a world-famous pop star and her backing-dancer husband, Xanadu loved to be the centre of attention. Everything about his appearance, from the tip of his bleached white

Mohican to the ends of his polished blue nails, screamed, "Look at me!". At the age of seven Xanadu had been given his own TV show, *Xanadu's World*, in which he'd travelled the planet in search of new dance moves. Among his more famous discoveries were the Brazilian Crossed Banana Splits and the Sichuan Shimmyhip. Personally, Bruno thought both moves made Xanadu look like a donkey trying to hold in its pee. In recent years, the child star had disappeared from the nation's TV screens. Now he claimed to be on the brink of making a comeback.

Grace rolled her eyes as the singing got louder and louder. "Just ignore him," she said.

"Oh, I'm taking it as a compliment," said Bruno. "Musical parping is my special talent, you know."

Grace's eyes widened. Bruno kicked himself. He should have known a swotty girl like her would disapprove. But then suddenly two dimples, like bites in an apple, appeared in her cheeks.

"That's the coolest thing ever!" she exclaimed.

"Really?" asked Bruno. "You really think so?" Grace nodded. Bruno grinned from ear to sticky-out ear.

"Well, thanks. It's great to meet someone

who gets how gifted I am." The singing had now reached a crescendo. Bruno twisted round in his seat and leant out into the aisle. "Hey, Xanadu!" he called. "I reckon that might be your first hit! Remind me again, how many people downloaded your last single?"

Xanadu's last single had sold only two copies, one to his mum and one to his grandma. He stopped singing as abruptly as if Bruno had pulled the plug out of the stereo.

Grace started to giggle. "You know, apart from Miss Goodwin, you're the first nice person I've met since coming to St Ermingarda's."

"Same here." Bruno smiled. "How about we stick together from now on?"

Grace grinned shyly back at him. "I'd like that."

By now the plane had begun its descent. The Mediterranean Sea stretched out below them like a shimmering blue cloth. Bruno felt his ears pop as the pilot turned sharply inland. He looked out of the window and saw that they were flying low over olive groves and vineyards. A minute or so later, the St Ermingarda's school jet touched down at an airfield just outside the glamorous seaside resort of Cannes. The sun was high in the sky, and stepping off the plane felt like stepping into a lovely warm bath. A fleet of limousines waited at the end of the runway, engines purring, ready to whisk the children away to their luxury hotel.

A few hours ago, Bruno had been determined to hate every second of the dreaded school trip. Now, with a new friend to share it with, he couldn't help but feel just a teeny-weeny bit excited.

6

The Hotel Magnificent

While an army of maids set to work unpacking suitcases, Miss Goodwin gathered her pupils together in a quiet corner of the Hotel Magnificent's private terrace. Palm trees swayed in the breeze. An Olympic-sized swimming pool glittered in the midday sun. Grace took a seat on a lounger next to Bruno, her eyes full of wonder.

"Have you ever seen anything like it?" she said. "The bathroom's five times bigger than my bedroom at home. They've folded the end of the loo paper into a triangle, just to make it look pretty. Can you believe it? Origami loo paper! That's what I call luxury!"

Miss Goodwin clapped her hands for silence. She had changed into a daisy-print sundress, crochet shawl and floppy straw hat. Already, freckles, like a dusting of cinnamon, had sprinkled themselves over her nose.

"Welcome to the sunny South of France," she said with a girlish pirouette. "Now before we all get too excited, we must try to remember that this trip is not just a holiday, but an *important learning opportunity.*"

The children gave a collective groan. Miss Goodwin's smile remained undimmed.

"As you know, for the past two terms we've been studying the medium of cinema. You've learnt about method acting and the technical skills of lighting and editing. We've covered everything from silent movies to spaghetti westerns. The time has come for you to put all that knowledge to the test. Over the next five days you won't just be watching films: you'll be making them. Working in pairs, your challenge is to produce a short documentary on a subject which I'm sure is close to all your hearts: *Fame: is it really all it's cracked up to be?* The best film will premier here at the festival on the last night of our trip."

A rare murmur of interest went around the class. Miss Goodwin was right. Fame was something her pupils knew a lot about. Xanadu wasn't the only one who saw more of his parents on the television than he did at home.

"Want to be partners?" Bruno asked Grace.

She gave an awkward shrug. "I'm not sure," she said. "You'd probably be better off with someone else. Fame isn't really something I know much about. I'm just – you know – normal."

"Don't be an idiot!" Bruno laughed. "That's what's so great about you."

The other children were also busy arranging themselves into pairs. Nobody wanted to go with Humbert. He stood beneath a palm tree, scowling at anyone who dared look in his direction. In the end, Miss Goodwin said that he should make up a three with Xanadu and a girl called Natasha Oblonsky.

As far as Bruno was concerned, the trio deserved each other.

Natasha was the only daughter of a Russian oil baron and a prima ballerina. Her toes were always pointed and her lips always pursed. She wore her long black hair in a plait trussed up with tartan ribbons, which swung behind her like the tail on an over-groomed pony. Although she tried her best not to show it, even Miss Goodwin was a little unnerved by the girl's coldly sophisticated manner. As Natasha liked to boast, there was not a five-star hotel that she had not stayed in. Nor a designer dress she wanted that she did not own. The world was Natasha Oblonsky's playground, and yet she always managed to look bored. Having to work in a group with Humbert and Xanadu should give her something to really sulk about for a change, thought Bruno.

"Does anyone have any questions?" asked Miss Goodwin.

Natasha tapped her foot, pouting until she got the teacher's attention. Why she couldn't just put her hand up like everyone else, Bruno would never understand.

"Go ahead," said Miss Goodwin with a nod.

"Film-making sounds like a cool assignment," admitted the young heiress, "but how are we supposed to make a film about fame with you tagging along? No offence, Miss Goodwin, but that sundress is not exactly stylish."

For the first time that day, the smile dimmed on Miss Goodwin's face. She fiddled nervously with one of the straps of her dress, then pulled her shawl tight about her chest.

"No offence taken, Natasha," she stuttered unconvincingly. "Actually, you'll be pleased to know that for once I won't be 'tagging along' beside you. The headmistress and I have agreed that on this occasion you will be allowed to work unsupervised."

The children gawped at each other in surprise. St Ermingarda's prided itself on allowing pupils a high degree of independence, but they were never usually allowed to do anything completely on their own.

"On one condition," added Miss Goodwin, raising her voice above the excited chatter. "Other than during our organized outings, all filming is to take place within the grounds of the hotel. Just obey that one little rule, and you will be fine. And before any of you rascals decide to sneak off to the beach, be warned. I'll be on the prowl to check up on you. Right then, if there are no more questions, could one person from each pair come forward and collect a camera and a microphone."

Now I think it's time to let you in on a little secret. A few tables away, unnoticed by anyone but you and me, a man with a handlebar moustache sat listening with interest. He was dressed in a three-piece suit and polka-dot cravat. At the man's side crouched a large white dog. This dog was rather unusual to look at, with long droopy ears and a fleshy brown nose. Two enormous nostrils twitched greedily at the air as the dog strained on her leash. The man was observing her behaviour with a mounting sense of excitement. Could it really be that after all these weeks spent combing the countryside, finally they'd found the very thing they were looking for, here at the hotel?

"Well, well, well, Trumpet," he muttered to the dog. "Who'd have thought it? Right under our noses!"

With any luck, one of these children was about to make the man with the handlebar moustache a very rich man indeed. He reached into his pocket for his mobile phone. It was time to give the duke some good news...

*   *   *

Later that same afternoon, Bruno and Grace were
huddled beneath a sunshade sharing a watermelon
sorbet. Bruno had just finished demonstrating his
technique for trumping a tune on demand and now
they were trying to come up with a winning idea for
their film project. Grace chewed on the end of her
pencil. Bruno screwed up his face, thinking as hard
as he could. It was no use. His mind was as blank as
an exercise book on the first morning of term.

"What I don't get," he grumbled, "is how *we're*
supposed to compete with *that*?"

Tilting back her hat, Grace scanned the terrace.
It didn't take her long to work out who Bruno was
talking about. While the majority of their classmates
were scattered about in little groups jotting down
ideas, Humbert and Natasha had changed into
their swimming things and were splashing about
in the pool. Xanadu lay sunning himself on a neon
pink lilo. He was wearing a pair of gold-spangled
swimming trunks. His ice-white Mohican had been
pushed forward into an Elvis-style quiff and he was
sipping from a luridly coloured mocktail.

"It's not fair," moaned Bruno. "All Natasha and
Humbert have to do is point the camera at Xanadu

and they'll have their film in no time."

Grace rubbed at an angry patch of skin on her arm. "But life's not fair, is it? I wouldn't worry. Humbert and Natasha are way too big-headed to film just Xanadu. They'll probably spend the whole time arguing about who gets the starring..."

Grace broke off mid-sentence. Her mouth fell open in the shape of an "O". In fact, a hush had fallen over the entire terrace. Guests stopped their conversations. Waiters stood rooted to the spot. Swimmers paused mid-stroke. Even the water in the fountains seemed to hang suspended in the air. Bruno looked about in confusion. Then, suddenly, he understood.

Floating through this frozen world, like a mermaid carried aloft on a wave, came a woman so gorgeous she barely seemed real. She was dressed in a sheaf of purple chiffon. Her hair tumbled down her back like yards of golden silk. Bruno did a double take. It couldn't be, could it? Surely not! Oh my goodness, it really was!

Her name was Desiree Draws. Star of such blockbuster movies as *Tarantulas Gone Wild, When Nuns Attack* and *Zombies in Bikinis: The Sequel.* By Bruno's calculations, she had to be one of the top ten most famous people on the whole planet!

There are times in life when the opportunity we've been waiting for catches us unprepared to take it. Then we spend the next day kicking ourselves as to what could have been. Bruno was determined that this should not be one of those occasions. Snatching up the microphone and camera, he jumped down from his seat.

"What are you doing?" asked Grace, snapping out of her trance.

"I'm going to ask her for an interview!" cried Bruno.

"You're crazy!" said Grace. "She'll never speak to us. She's one of the most famous women in the—"

But it was too late. Bruno was already tearing across the terrace towards Ms Draws. The ribbon of his straw hat fluttered as he ran, dodging this way and that between sun loungers and umbrellas. All he had to do was get her to answer a couple of questions on camera and they'd be sure to win the prize for the best documentary. Here was his chance to carry out the assignment *and* make his Grandpa Trevor proud.

7

The Great Producer

Desiree Draws swept into the lobby of the Hotel Magnificent. Bruno followed just a few metres behind. He looked about in awe. The painted silk wallpaper, the onyx skirting boards and cabinets inlaid with mother-of-pearl were dazzling to behold, and the air was perfumed with lilies. Desiree had paused in the middle of the room and was checking a message on her phone. Bruno gulped. He racked his brains for something clever to say. Then, just as he was about to enter the star's orbit, a most unexpected thing happened.

A huge white dog appeared from nowhere, bounding across the lobby and skidding on the marble tiles. When it reached Bruno, the dog ran round and round his feet, sniffing excitedly at the hem of his shorts. At first it was as if the dog was painting a kiss with the brush of her tail. Then Bruno felt the wind knocked out of him. Two fat paws landed squarely on his chest and sent him toppling to the floor. Bruno struggled to get up again, but it was no use. The mighty mutt had him pinned firmly to the ground. All Bruno could do was watch helplessly as Desiree Draws disappeared out through a revolving glass door. He'd missed his chance.

The dog's breath was uncomfortably warm and meaty. Bruno closed his eyes as a glistening ribbon of drool detached itself from the slobbering jaws and fell slowly towards his face.

When Bruno wiped away the drool and blinked open his eyes, he recognized only one of the two faces staring down at him. That face belonged to Grace Chalk. To Bruno's annoyance, dimples had appeared in her cheeks and her skin was flushed red with laughter. The face he didn't recognize belonged to a man with an enormous handlebar moustache. The man crouched down and clipped a heavy gold lead onto the dog's collar. His oiled hair was dyed jet black and he spoke in a peculiar sing-song voice.

"Oh my, oh my, I do apologize. It seems
Trumpet has taken something of a shine to you.
Perhaps we might call it love at first sniff!"

Bruno watched in a daze as the man heaved on
the lead. Strangely, given the heat,
he was dressed in a three-piece
suit and a polka-dot cravat.
Tucked beneath his right
arm was a gold and ivory
tipped cane.

At last the dog's paws lifted from Bruno's chest,
her tail waving like a victory flag as she went to sit
at her master's side. Bruno waited until the air had
returned to his lungs, then hauled himself to his

feet. "Maybe you should try keeping your dog on the lead next time." He knew he sounded rude, but the stupid dog had ruined everything.

"Don't be like that," said Grace and bent down to ruffle the dog's droopy white ears. "Trumpet was only trying to be friendly, weren't you, Trumpet? Besides, a superstar like Desiree Draws would never have spoken to us anyway."

The man with the handlebar moustache looked worried. He twirled his cane about in little circles as if stirring the water in an invisible pond.

"I do hope Trumpet's display of affection hasn't inconvenienced you somehow?" The dog rolled over on its back, offering Grace its tummy to tickle.

"It was only a silly idea for a school project," she said, rubbing Trumpet's belly. "We're supposed to be making a documentary about fame. Bruno thought he'd get an interview from Desiree Draws. As if that'd ever happen!"

Bruno felt a wave of indignation. It wasn't a silly idea, it was a good idea. And if it wasn't for the blasted dog, they'd have won the film competition for sure.

Grace was still stroking the dog's tummy,

chattering away happily to the strange man. Something about the dog's presence seemed to help her overcome her shyness.

"I'm not really supposed to touch animals. It sets my allergies off. But I don't mind. Animals are a lot nicer than most humans, don't you think? What kind of breed is Trumpet, anyway? Is she a kind of spaniel? I've always wanted one of those."

The man with the handlebar moustache let out a high-pitched squeaking laugh.

"A spaniel? Heavens, no! Trumpet is the finest example of a Trumpenhund that you will ever meet."

"A Trumpenhund?" repeated Bruno. "I've never heard of one of those before."

"Oh, but they're very rare," explained the man. "Rarer than a carnivorous rabbit! And one hundred times more dangerous, too!"

Bruno shivered as he remembered the sight of the dog's slobbery jaws hovering above his face.

"Only joking!" shrieked the man. "Trumpet's as gentle as a newborn lamb."

He patted the dog's head, then studied the children thoughtfully, as if something had just occurred to him. He caressed the waves of hair above his lip. "You're doing a school project about fame, you said?"

Grace nodded.

"Ooh-la-la! This might just be your lucky day!" He tumbled forward into an elaborate bow. "Please allow me the pleasure of introducing myself..." Reaching into the pocket of his waistcoat, the man pulled out a little white business card, which he handed to Grace.

"*Monsieur Zachary Zidler*," she read out loud. "*Impresario.*"

Monsieur Zidler snapped himself back upright. "At your service!" he declared.

Not quite sure what to do with the card, Grace shoved it into the inside pocket of her blazer.

"Pleased to meet you," she said, shyly offering her hand to shake. "I'm Grace Chalk, and this is my friend Bruno Pockley."

"Im-pre-sa-rio?" said Bruno, struggling to pronounce the word. "What does that mean?"

"It's a posh name for someone who puts on concerts or plays," explained Grace.

"Oh yeah, of course." Bruno blushed. "I knew that."

Monsieur Zidler bent down until his face was

53

level with the children's. Up close, his teeth were startlingly white and his moustache smelt of powdered violets.

"My dears," he whispered smoothly, "the word means so much more than that."

Bruno could see that Grace, who prided herself on having a large vocabulary, was a little put out at being corrected. Monsieur Zidler drew himself back up to his full height.

"Some people call me *The Great Producer*," he announced grandly. "But you should think of me as a kind of talent scout. In fact, it might just interest you to know that I'm here at the festival looking for children to cast in my next production. Forget about school projects! Forget about Ms Draws! If I choose, I can make you the most famous children in the universe!"

Bruno and Grace looked at each other in astonishment. Could the man be serious?

"Just imagine it!" cried Zidler, pointing his cane at the ceiling. "Your faces beaming out from the cover of every magazine! Your names in lights on billboards twelve metres high!"

Bruno was starting to like the sound of this. "You could really arrange all that?" he asked.

Monsieur Zidler's smile was almost as broad as his moustache. "That's nothing!" he declared. "Stick with me, and I shall have you blasted into the stars!" By now, even Trumpet was panting with excitement. Then Monsieur Zidler's expression became serious.

"There is, of course, the small matter of an audition in front of my associates. But details-shmetails! For two such charming children as yourselves the audition should prove no problem. What do you say we meet outside the front of the hotel at half past five tomorrow morning? I'll take you on a journey that'll put an end to life as you know it!"

Bruno did not need to think about his answer. "Sounds great! We'll see you there."

Grace was tugging on the sleeve of his shirt.

"What?" he asked, a little impatiently.

She pointed out to the terrace, where Miss Goodwin was sitting with her nose wedged between the pages of a book.

"We're not supposed to leave the hotel. It's the one thing Miss Goodwin asked us not to do. She's trusting us."

Bruno pulled a face. Did Grace always have

to be so sensible? "You don't think Humbert and Natasha are going to play by the rules, do you?"

"I guess not," Grace admitted. "Still, it doesn't feel right."

Monsieur Zidler took a step back. His face was all sympathy and understanding.

"Perhaps I should leave you to discuss this little matter between yourselves. I have no desire to put any pressure upon you."

He gave another extravagant bow, then turned on his heel and sauntered away through the lobby. The Trumpenhund trotted along at her master's side. Like a pair of windscreen wipers on a rainy day, the dog's tail and the man's gold-tipped cane seemed to move together in perfect time.

Just before they disappeared out of earshot, Bruno called after them. "We'll be there. I promise!"

The next thing that happened was that Bruno and Grace had their first argument. In fact, it was the only true quarrel they would ever have. I won't go into the details of who said what to whom, for that would be really quite boring. As in most arguments, they simply went round and round, each repeating their point of view over and over, getting more and more frustrated that the other wouldn't see sense. In a nutshell, their disagreement was this: Bruno thought that they should meet Monsieur Zidler in the morning. Grace didn't.

"We'll get expelled," she protested. "I'll lose my scholarship."

"Don't be such a goody two-shoes," Bruno retaliated. "Forget school! We're going to be famous!"

"Famous for what?" demanded Grace.

Bruno just about resisted the urge to stamp his foot. Why did Grace have to be so pernickety?

"Who cares?" he burst out. "It's the being famous that counts! Do you really want to stay a nobody for ever? Don't you want to make your parents proud?"

Parents. Bruno felt a rush of sadness as he said the word. It was too late for him to impress his mum and dad. Still, it would mean so much to Grandpa Trevor if Bruno was to become a star.

In the end, it was Grace who caved in. She still had her doubts, of course, but she hated arguing.

"All right," she conceded. "I'll come with you to

the audition. But we'd better be back before anyone notices."

"I swear on my grandpa's life, if we get caught, I'll say it was all my fault and that I made you do it," promised Bruno. "And anyway, they'd never expel you. You're Miss Goodwin's star pupil. The worst you'd ever get is a Saturday detention."

Later, Bruno would come to wish he'd listened to Grace. For as you will know, it is a golden rule never to go off with strangers. Monsieur Zidler may well have been an impresario with a fancy business card and an even fancier moustache, but he was a stranger nonetheless.

8

A Ride into the Country

That night, Bruno could barely sleep a wink.
The bed was the softest he had ever lain on. The
pillows were the fluffiest he had ever touched.
Yet still the hours of darkness seemed to drag on
for ever. As soon as the bedside clock read 05:00,
Bruno was out of his bed and into his school
uniform. Thinking it might be good to make a bit
of an effort for the audition, he sprinkled some
water onto his mop of brown curls. But no matter
how often he wrestled it down, his hair just sprang
straight back up again.

As satisfied as he could be with his appearance,
Bruno crept out into the corridor and went to

knock for Grace. When there was no answer, he paced back and forth, itching with impatience. From a nearby room came the sound of a toilet flushing. Somewhere, someone switched on a television. For some strange reason, a few of the other children seemed to be stirring. Bruno couldn't wait much longer. If Grace didn't appear soon, he'd have to go to meet Monsieur Zidler on his own.

Just as Bruno was about to give up on her, Grace popped her head out into the corridor. Her eyes were as round as golf balls as she looked to the left and to the right to check that no one was coming.

"I can't believe I let you talk me into this," she whispered, shutting the door quietly behind her. "We're going to get in so–o–o–o much trouble."

"You worry too much," Bruno dismissed. "Now, come on, quick!"

The lift doors pinged open. Save for a night porter snoozing behind the reception desk, the lobby was empty. Being careful not to wake him, Bruno and Grace crept out through the revolving glass door. Outside, a street sweeper was hard at work cleaning up the rubbish left over from last night's film parties. Champagne corks and broken glass littered the pavements. A gaggle of seagulls fought over a discarded feather boa, thinking it might make a nice lining for a nest. There was no sign of Monsieur Zidler.

Grace glanced anxiously at her watch. The sun had not yet warmed the sky and her arms were bristling with goosebumps.

"We are a bit early," she said with a shiver. "I just hope he gets here before anyone spots us leaving the hotel."

Though he didn't admit it, Bruno was nervous too. What if Monsieur Zidler had forgotten about their meeting? What if he'd found some other children to make famous?

The seconds ticked by.

At last they heard the swish of a revolving door behind them. Bruno felt a wave of relief. Yet when the door swung round, it wasn't Monsieur Zidler who tumbled out, but Humbert, Natasha and Xanadu. Even at this ungodly hour, Xanadu was wearing his shades.

"Wassup, dudes?" he yawned, before wandering off to admire his reflection in the bonnet of a shiny red Ferrari.

The other children eyeballed each other with suspicion.

"What are you two doing here?" asked Natasha. She couldn't have sounded more disgusted if she'd found two pieces of chewing gum stuck to her shoe.

"Hanging around like a bad smell as usual," Humbert sneered.

Bruno puffed out his chest like a pigeon. "Well, if you must know, Grace and I are here to— Ouch! What did you do that for?"

For some reason Grace had decided to step on his foot.

"I thought we agreed to keep it a secret," she whispered.

"A secret." Natasha rolled the word about on her tongue. "Hmm, let me guess, what could it be? I know! The scholarship kids are here to earn some extra money by helping to clean the streets. That's what your dad does, isn't it, Grace? Isn't he a dustman?"

Grace's green eyes narrowed. It was the first time Bruno had ever seen her look angry.

"So what if he is," she said, clenching her small white fists. "At least he isn't killing penguins and fouling up the seas with his dirty great oil rigs."

It seemed that although she was quite happy to laugh at Grace's father, Natasha did not appreciate it when the tables were turned. She began to swear violently in her mother tongue. Bruno had no idea what she was saying, which is just as well, since the insults streaming from his classmate's pursed pink lips were far too rude to reprint here. Grace, on the other hand, seemed to understand perfectly. The boys looked on in astonishment as the two girls squared up to each other, cursing in Russian. Bruno couldn't believe it. This was not the shy, retiring Grace Chalk he knew.

Just in time to stop a full-blown fight from breaking out, Monsieur Zidler screeched up in a pea-green sports car. The car looked very expensive, with a fold-down roof and a red leather interior. Trumpet was perched on the passenger seat, and when she caught sight of the children, she let out a yelp of joy. Monsieur Zidler seemed equally pleased to see them.

"Oh my, oh my, how wonderful!" he cried, switching off the engine and hurrying round to greet them. "You're all here."

"W-w-what do you mean?" stammered Bruno.

63

"I thought you were only expecting me and
Grace?"

Monsieur Zidler brought his hands together in
the manner of a vicar about to offer an important
lesson.

"I'm afraid that since I wasn't entirely sure you
were coming, I had no choice but to scout about
for a few alternatives. The more the merrier, don't
you think?" He held open the back door of the car.
"In you hop. Bit of a squeeze, but I'm sure you're all
good friends."

Xanadu jumped straight into the car, swiftly
followed by a disgruntled Bruno. Natasha flicked
her hair and fluttered her lashes and flashed her
best fake smile at Monsieur Zidler. Then she
carefully placed her bottom on the leather seat

before swinging in
her legs, just as
her Russian
governess had
taught her a
lady must do.

Unimpressed by this little performance, Humbert stood sour-faced and scowling on the pavement.

"I want to go in the front," he demanded. "It's stupid that the dog gets the best seat. Dogs should go in the boot."

Monsieur Zidler frowned. "In the boot? Well, I'm afraid that won't be possible. Of course, *you* can always travel in the boot if you wish. But the front seat is reserved for Trumpet."

Still scowling, Humbert clambered into the back. As he passed behind the dog, he reached out and yanked down hard on her ear. Trumpet let out a yelp of pain. She jumped up and bared her sharp white teeth at Humbert, growling furiously.

Now only Grace remained on the pavement. Monsieur Zidler offered her a gloved hand to help her into the car, but Grace did not take it. Instead, she stared down at the ground. Her voice was quiet but determined.

"I'm sorry, but I've changed my mind. I can't come with you." She looked up at her classmates. There was a note of warning in her voice. "Miss Goodwin is going to be really cross about this."

All the other children groaned.

Monsieur Zidler rested a hand on Grace's shoulder. His face was the picture of concern.

"My dear child, didn't I mention that I had a long chat with your teacher last night at the hotel bar? No? Why, how silly of me. It must have been all that wine we drank. Miss Goodwin thought it was a wonderful idea for you to come away with me for a few days. In fact she said the auditions would be 'an important learning opportunity'."

Grace frowned. That did sound just like Miss Goodwin. She was a little surprised to hear they'd be away for a few days, but if going to the auditions was OK with their teacher, what could be the harm?

"Of course," Monsieur Zidler added, "you can always stay behind if you prefer."

Grace shook her head as she squeezed in beside Humbert. "If Miss Goodwin's happy, I'd love to come."

Monsieur Zidler scurried round to the front and slipped into the driver's seat. There was no more time for second thoughts. The key turned in the ignition and the engine roared into life. With a screech of tyres, they were off!

*　　*　　*

Trumpet's ears blew back in the breeze as her master slammed his foot against the accelerator. They raced along the seafront, away from the centre of town, down an avenue of palm trees.

"Hold onto your hats!" cried Monsieur Zidler, but it was too late. The wind had whipped the children's straw boaters from their heads. They flew off in all directions like seed scattering from a dandelion clock.

"Woo-hoo!" shouted Bruno. "This is the life."

Back at the hotel, Miss Goodwin stirred gently in her sleep. She stretched out an arm, then nuzzled into the duvet, dreaming sweet dreams of a chance encounter with a handsome young man on horseback. A battered copy of *Jane Eyre* lay open on the bed beside her. The book was an old favourite of hers, full of romance and mystery. After seeing all the children to bed, she'd headed straight up to her room and read into the small hours.

Bless her, she looks so pretty in her frilly pink nightie – and so peaceful, with her honey-coloured hair spilling over the pillow. Let us tiptoe away and leave her slumbering there for an hour or so longer.

9

The Knights Trumplar

The pea-green sports car sped on through a cloud of dust. Xanadu led the children in a rowdy chorus from *Fame*, complete with coordinated dance moves. They waved their hands from left to right. They rolled their fists one over the other, like a whirring tombola. They threw their arms above their heads, then waggled their fingers (ta-da!) as if jumping out from a cake. Something about the breeze in their hair, and being on a journey to who knew where, seemed to help them forget about their differences, at least for a while.

Monsieur Zidler had soon turned away from the coast and now they were heading up, up, into the hills. Here, simple farmsteads crouched among pastures and meadows. The farmers were away in their fields or busy milking cows in cow barns. To the lone goatherd who watched the sports car pass, they looked much like any other strange city folk off to spend a day in the country. He chuckled to himself at the children's eccentric school uniforms and marvelled at the majesty of their driver's moustache. Only the next evening, when he turned on the television in his lonely goat hut, would he realize that he'd witnessed a dangerous kidnapper making off with his prey.

Bruno waited for a lull in the singing, then leant forward and tapped Monsieur Zidler on the shoulder. He had to shout to be heard above the wind. "Excuse me, but where are we going?"

"Say that again!" bellowed Monsieur Zidler. "I couldn't hear you!"

"I SAID, WHERE ARE WE GOING?"

Monsieur Zidler wound up his window and gestured for the children to do the same. He pushed a button below the steering wheel and the fold-down roof reared up behind their heads then clanked down over the top of the car. The roar of the wind was silenced. Suddenly they could hear themselves think.

"You had a question for me, Bruno?" asked Monsieur Zidler.

"I was just wondering where we're going? You said something yesterday about an audition in front of" – Bruno tried to remember Monsieur Zidler's exact words – "your associates?"

"Did I, now?" Monsieur Zidler twiddled the end of his moustache. "Then I'd say it was time for a little lesson in history, wouldn't you, Trumpet?"

Woof, woof, barked the dog, thumping her paws against the dashboard.

"Boring!" chimed Natasha and Xanadu together.

Monsieur Zidler swung round to face them. As his eyes left the road, the car swerved dangerously to the right. They were now bumping along with two wheels up on the rocky verge, but their driver didn't seem to notice.

"Boring?" he cried. "That depends on what you think of riches and glory and fame and immeasurable fortune."

Just in time to avoid crashing into a giant pine tree, Monsieur Zidler returned his gaze to the front. The children let out a collective sigh of relief as the car lurched back into the centre of the road.

Grace plucked up the courage to ask another question.

"But what does history have to do with where we're going for our audition?"

"My dear child, it has everything to do with it." This time Monsieur Zidler managed to keep his eyes on the road. They glittered like diamonds in the rear-view mirror. "Listen carefully, children, and I shall tell you…"

The speech that followed was peppered with whinnies and giggles, as if words alone could not communicate Monsieur Zidler's excitement.

He spoke of a time when brotherhoods of knights had roamed the whole of Europe. He told how these brave men had risked life and limb to glorify their rulers. Some fought wars in the name of religion; others slew dragons and rescued damsels in distress. There were those, he said, of whom the children might already have heard. Like Arthur, who drew the sword from the stone. Or the Knights Templar, who invented banks and bailed out popes and emperors.

"But one group has been erased from the history books!" exclaimed Monsieur Zidler. "They did not trade in religion or violence or bank loans! Oh no, their activities were far more glamorous. They are the knights whose exploits have been kept hidden beneath a cloak of secrecy. They excel in making people famous, and their name is … the Knights Trumplar!"

"The *who*?" asked all his passengers together.

Monsieur Zidler dropped his voice to an intoxicating whisper. The children jostled forward in their seats, hanging on his every word.

"The Knights Trumplar is a highly secretive organization. For centuries they controlled the flow of fame around the world. Their scouts plucked talented children from obscurity, trained them until they were flawless, then catapulted them onto the stage. So grateful were these children that they pledged a portion of their earnings to the knights for ever. Over time the knights became richer than the kings and queens they were intended to serve. Fearing a threat to their power, the monarchy had them exiled from their lands. Many were murdered. Those who escaped fled up into the mountains, where they were given shelter by their one remaining ally, the ruler of an ancient Alpine kingdom known as Phartesia. They made him their leader, and there they live to this day, quietly pulling the strings and oiling the cogs of that great machine known as Celebrity. There's not a blockbuster movie, nor a bestselling album, that cannot be traced back to their training or their money. For, you see, the Knights Trumplar did not vanish or lose their power, they simply went underground. Soon, you yourselves will have the opportunity to audition in front of them."

The children looked at each other in wonder. Could this really be true? A secret organization that helped make people famous? Monsieur Zidler seemed deadly serious. Deciding that they did indeed believe him, the children whooped and cheered. Even Natasha deigned to clap her hands.

"Jeepers!" cried Bruno, suddenly guessing the answer to his original question. "So does that mean we're going to Phartesia?"

"What a clever child you are!" said Monsieur Zidler, beaming at Bruno in the rear-view mirror. The reflection of his bright white teeth was dazzling.

Just at that moment, a jagged mountain range, wreathed in cloud and capped with snow, appeared on the horizon. A trio of buzzards circled overhead as Monsieur Zidler put down the roof and sped on towards the tallest mountain of them all.

10

Panic at the Hotel Magnificent

And now I think it's time we woke Miss Goodwin. We'll let her have a shower, brush her teeth and pick out a sundress. (Recalling Natasha's hurtful remark, she decides against a rose-print pinafore and opts instead for chic grey linen.) But sooner or later we will have to tell her the bad news.

Do you want to break it to her, or shall I?

It won't be pretty.

Oh, all right, then, I suppose I'd better do it.

Feeling relaxed about the day ahead, Miss Goodwin picked up her register and strolled out into the corridor. By now her pupils should have received their wake-up calls. With a bit of luck they'd already be downstairs, stuffing their faces from the hotel buffet.

Sure enough, when she entered the glass-walled dining room, Miss Goodwin spotted a swarm of children in purple blazers buzzing around a table piled high with pastries. She did a quick head count. Five members of her class were missing. The teacher was not too worried. It was normal for there to be a few stragglers. All Miss Goodwin had to do (or so she thought) was go upstairs and chivvy them out of their rooms. It was only when she checked against her register and noticed that Grace Chalk was among those absent that she felt a tiny twinge of anxiety. It was not like Grace to be late for anything. Telling herself not to be such a worrier, Miss Goodwin took the lift back up to the third floor. She banged on one door after another. When each child failed to answer, she let herself into their room with an electronic swipe card. It was the same story in every room: the beds had been slept in, but the children were nowhere to be seen. Miss Goodwin tried not to panic. Maybe she'd missed them coming up in the lift.

Yet to her dismay, when she went back

downstairs there was still no sign of them in the dining room.

An early morning swim! That must be it, she thought, running out onto the terrace. She would have to get cross. They were not supposed to go in the water without adult supervision. But the surface of the pool was still and unruffled. Nor was there any sign of the children in the games room. Dashing back into the dining room, Miss Goodwin began to quiz the rest of her class. Had they seen Grace or Natasha, Humbert or Bruno or Xanadu?

"No, miss," they said through mouthfuls of pain au chocolat.

"Are you sure?" she pressed. "Are you one hundred per cent sure you haven't seen them?"

Still munching, the children shook their heads.

Miss Goodwin turned her attention to the other diners. She moved desperately from table to table.

"Can anyone help me?" she pleaded. "I'm looking for some children. About the same height as those ones over there. There's one boy with a Mohican and sunglasses – you couldn't miss him. A boy with a thin little face and a girl with her hair all done up in ribbons. Another boy who looks – well, sort of scruffy. Oh, and Grace Chalk, who wouldn't say boo to a goose. Surely somebody must have seen something!"

The guests turned their heads away or hid behind their morning papers. As if it wasn't bad enough having to share the hotel with a bunch of noisy school kids, now this madwoman wanted to interrupt their breakfast.

Miss Goodwin tried again. "Please," she begged a woman who was staring pointedly up at the ceiling. "Are you *sure* you haven't seen them?"

The woman refused to meet her eye. Miss Goodwin wished she could shake her until the answer came rattling out like coins from a piggy bank. But that would be illegal, and Miss Goodwin had never done anything illegal.

Instead, she began to hyperventilate. Each quick, shallow breath deprived her blood of oxygen and increased her panic. Her head swam. Feeling giddy, she clutched at the table for support.

It rocked. Coffee pots and crockery went toppling over. The woman leapt from her seat, outraged.

"This madwoman is trying to attack me!" she screamed.

"Excuse me, madame, but may I be of assistance?"

Miss Goodwin felt a pair of firm hands grasp the small of her waist. She took a deep breath. At last, someone who wanted to help. She turned to see the familiar face of Monsieur Petit, the hotel manager. With his clipped grey beard and badger-streaked hair he was hardly a handsome young man on horseback, but he would have to do. She allowed herself to be steered away from the table.

"Perhaps we might step into my office?"

"What?" gasped Miss Goodwin, who was still trying to catch her breath. "Oh no, that's terribly kind, but I couldn't abandon my pupils."

"Really, madame, I'm afraid I must insist." He lowered his voice. "You're causing a scene."

Miss Goodwin did not appreciate the hotel manager's tone. For once in her life she decided to get strict. She wagged her finger in Monsieur Petit's face.

"Causing a scene? Of course I am causing

78

a scene, you nincompoop! Five children have gone missing and all anyone cares about is their croissants! I insist that you take charge and call the police at once!"

"Certainly, madame," said the hotel manager. He gave a curt little nod. Two burly security guards appeared from behind a potted fern. They hooked their arms beneath Miss Goodwin's armpits and hoisted her into the air.

"Stop! Stop!" The teacher kicked and screamed. "Whatever do you think you're doing? Take your hands off me at once or I shall be forced to..." She searched for something threatening to say. "Erm, I shall be forced to bite you!"

But the security guards may as well have been tasked with removing a feather. They carried Miss Goodwin out into the corridor and bundled her into a lift.

It is a fact known only to a few people that on the twenty-seventh floor of the Hotel Magnificent there is a solid steel room. This room is located to the right of the penthouse suite and measures nine metres square. It is fitted with CCTV and a bombproof door. Designed first and foremost as a safe haven for celebrities in the event of an attempted kidnapping, the room can also serve as a prison cell.

It was to this room that Monsieur Petit and his security guards escorted Miss Goodwin. Pushing her inside, they slammed the door shut behind her. Monsieur Petit turned to the taller of the guards.

"Ask the police to come and collect her when they get the chance. Oh, and do find a quiet room for those other children. They're making the place look untidy."

Miss Goodwin was hammering against the door. Her shouts were muffled by the steel walls but you could still make out the words.

"Let me out! You stupid meatheads! We're wasting precious time!"

"And for heaven's sake," the hotel manager said with a sigh, "turn the soundproofing on. We can't have this nutcase disturbing Ms Draws."

11

The Golden Gates

The pea-green sports car was now almost halfway up the mountain. It was cooler here in the forest. Light filtered down through the branches in lime-gold shafts. The air was thick with insects and midges. Everywhere there was the sound of water dripping. Sun melted the snow on the mountain top and the water flowed down in rivers, collecting in pools from which deer could sometimes be glimpsed drinking. In places, the water came tumbling over moss-covered rocks.

By now the children had been travelling for hours. They were not hungry, for Monsieur Zidler had stopped earlier to hand out a round of sandwiches. But they were bored and uncomfortable, squashed together in the back.

"This journey is taking for–ev–er," complained Xanadu.

"Hey, Mister Xylophone, or whatever your name is," Natasha demanded. "Are we nearly there yet, or what?"

"Yeah, Mister Zimmerframe," moaned Humbert. "How much longer till we get to Phartesia? All these waterfalls are making me want to pee!"

The man with the handlebar moustache was not amused. "My name," he insisted, "is Zidler. Monsieur Zachary Zidler. Otherwise known as The Great Producer, Talent Scout Extraordinaire and Master of Your Destiny. And what Monsieur Zidler can personally guarantee is that children who whinge do not become famous!"

A worse fate could not be imagined. Natasha and Xanadu stopped their complaining. Humbert crossed his legs.

Bruno and Grace could not resist a little smirk.

As it turned out, the children did not have much longer to wait. Soon the car rounded a bend in the road and an enormous stone gateway appeared among the trees. As they approached the gates, Bruno noticed that Grace seemed to be finding something very amusing. Two penny-sized dimples cut into her cheeks before she gave way to a fit of giggles.

"What's so funny?" asked Bruno.

"Look at that statue!" said Grace, pointing.

All the children craned their necks to see. One by one, they began to laugh. Perched atop the gateway was the bust of a man's head, which possessed an even more impressive moustache than Monsieur Zidler's. Each carved whisker spiralled down a full three metres to the ground, forming an archway through which visitors might enter.

The gates themselves were cast from solid gold and decorated with silver stars. Painted across them in swirling black letters was the word *Phartesia*.

Monsieur Zidler slowed the engine to a crawl, then pulled up beside a gold and white striped sentry box. The children's merriment turned to surprise as the door to the sentry box swung open and out popped two men in uniform. Like Monsieur Zidler and the statue, both of the sentries sported vast handlebar moustaches. Their uniform did not resemble the heavy armour you see in storybooks, nor was it like the camouflage gear you

see modern soldiers wearing. Instead they were dressed in blue-and-white silk doublets, with ruffed collars and turquoise silk tights. On their heads they wore purple hats shaped like flower pots. On their feet they wore hefty wooden clogs decorated with brightly coloured pompoms. The only thing about their attire that linked them to the knights the children had learnt about at school were the sharp swords glinting at their sides.

"Holy baloney," whispered Bruno to no one in particular, "these must be the Knights Trumplar!"

Monsieur Zidler beamed with pleasure. "Bravo! Well guessed, young man!"

The knights did not smile. They simply nodded at Monsieur Zidler, who rolled down his window and cried out in a strange hurdy-gurdy language, *"Al halicus ye Duck di Phartesia!"* (Or at least that's what it sounded like to the children.)

Trumpet barked, then raised one white paw in the air.

"Al halicus ye Duck di Phartesia!" echoed the knights and pushed back the heavy metal gates.

As they passed beneath the mighty stone moustache, Natasha turned to Grace with a sly look on her face.

"So, Little Miss Scholarship, if you're so great at languages, why don't you translate?"

Grace tucked her fringe behind her ear and spoke with quiet conviction.

"If you really want to know, they're speaking a Latinate language with influences of German and Sanskrit. What they said was: All hail the duck of Phartesia."

"Cool, man," enthused Xanadu.

Natasha let out a snort of derision.

"You can't seriously expect us to believe that," said Humbert scornfully.

"You can believe what you want," Grace replied with a shrug. "That's the translation."

The car rumbled on down the road. So this was Phartesia! Birds flittered in and out of the trees, thrushes and warblers and cuckoos and finches, all of them singing. Sprouting from among the gnarled roots of larch and elder trees were buttercups and bright purple orchids.

"I think we're going to like it here," said Bruno, smiling at Grace.

Not everyone was so impressed. Dotted among the trees were ramshackle huts. Ragged peasants crouched in the doorways, averting their eyes from the car as it passed.

"I hope Monsieur Zimmerframe realizes I won't stay anywhere that's not five-star," Natasha muttered to Humbert.

The words came out just a little louder than she had hoped.

"What's that?" snapped Monsieur Zidler, spinning round to face her. "Do I detect the sound of whingeing? Well, I think you'll find that the Castle Mistral is luxurious enough to suit even the most spoilt children."

A castle! The children sat up tall in their seats, each hoping they'd be the first to spy it.

Investigations Commence

Inspector Jacques Balzac stood looking at the TV screen with his hands knotted behind his back. He was a tall, thin man whose blond hair was slicked back in a single smooth wave. In his current posture he resembled a heron waiting patiently at the edge of a pond.

The fish Inspector Balzac had come to hook was not a big one. It had been a routine call-out to the Hotel Magnificent. A rowdy guest had been detained by security guards after smashing crockery in the hotel dining room. Such acts of vandalism were not unusual during the film festival, when people were apt to drink too many cocktails and make a nuisance of themselves. So routine, in fact, did this crime seem to Inspector Balzac that he had decided to stop for a spot of lunch before pottering over to investigate. Now he was standing in the dusty office of Monsieur Petit, the hotel manager, suffused in the warm glow that comes from having a bellyful of snails and claret.

He peered closely at the TV screen, scrutinizing every detail of the lone female suspect. Miss Goodwin, as he had already established the woman was named, had given up hammering at the walls and was now down on her hands and knees, feeling around the floor of her cell as if searching for a trapdoor.

"See what I mean?" said Monsieur Petit with a note of satisfaction in his voice. "A raving nutcase!"

But Inspector Balzac wasn't so sure. There was something about this woman that didn't add up. In his thirty-nine years of service to the French police force, Inspector Balzac had encountered every kind of criminal. From the bungling thief with bulging pockets to the cold-blooded killer who will never show remorse, Inspector Balzac had arrested them all. Somehow Miss Goodwin didn't strike him as the criminal type. It wasn't because she was pretty.

Often the pretty ones were the worst. It was just an instinct he had about her face. What's more, her cries of innocence struck him as genuine. He turned to the hotel manager.

"Remind me, why am I supposed to arrest her?"

Monsieur Petit cleared his throat. "It's very straightforward, inspector. She disturbed the peace in my dining room, then threatened to assault two of my security staff."

"Two burly security guards?" Inspector Balzac raised an eyebrow. "Assault them how, exactly?"

"Bite them," replied the hotel manager matter-of-factly.

The inspector let out a sigh as he took a pair of handcuffs from his pocket. "I suppose I shall have to bring her in for questioning."

"About time too," huffed Monsieur Petit, smoothing down the creases in his jacket.

Inspector Balzac paused in the doorway. "By the way, was there anything to prompt this outburst?"

"Oh, nothing relevant," said Monsieur Petit, ushering him out through the door. "Some hysterical nonsense about missing children. I checked with the other pupils and they'd only been gone an hour or so. Everyone knows kids go walkabout."

Inspector Balzac turned very slowly on his heel. His voice was dangerously soft.

"Say that again," he whispered.

"Everyone knows kids go walkabout," repeated the hotel manager, a hint of uncertainty creeping into his voice.

"Not that, you idiot!" bellowed Inspector Balzac. "The bit about the missing children!"

He barged back into the office and snatched at the calendar that hung above Monsieur Petit's desk. The dates were crossed off in red ink. Inspector Balzac paled.

"The thirteenth of May," he said, aghast. This was the date every policeman in Europe had learned to dread. "I don't believe it. He's struck again!"

"What are you talking about?" asked the hotel manager. "What don't you believe? *Who's* struck again?"

Inspector Balzac did not answer him. Instead he did something which took Monsieur Petit quite by surprise. He held out the handcuffs and slipped them around the hotel manager's wrists.

"Monsieur Petit," he announced, "I'm arresting you for obstructing a police investigation and for the unlawful detention of an innocent woman.

Now tell me where your keys are so I can go and unlock that poor teacher at once."

Half an hour later Miss Goodwin sat across a desk from Inspector Balzac at police headquarters. Monsieur Petit was also present, handcuffed and snivelling in the corner. Most of one wall was covered with a large white board, upon which lists of names and dates were scrawled in black marker pen. The remaining walls were covered with a rogue's gallery of criminals thought to be operating in the area.

Inspector Balzac took a slurp of coffee. "Let's go over your statement from the top, shall we, mademoiselle?"

Miss Goodwin nodded. Dark circles had appeared around her eyes. Her hands were bruised from hours of hammering.

"Five of your pupils are missing. You last saw them at nine o'clock yesterday evening when you tucked them safely into their beds. When the children failed to appear at breakfast this morning, you checked their rooms and found they were empty. You asked for help, but instead Monsieur Petit had you incarcerated. Is that all correct?"

Miss Goodwin confirmed that this was indeed all quite correct. Inspector Balzac rose from his chair. He strode over to the far side of the room.

"Now I need to know something from you, Monsieur Petit." He pointed at one of the mugshots pinned to the wall. "This man here. Do you recognize him?"

The mugshot was not a photograph but a sketched artist's impression. It showed a man with oiled hair and a handlebar moustache. It was not a perfect likeness. The nose was a bit bigger, the eyes a little closer together, and the forehead just a fraction too high. But still I'm sure you would have recognized the man as being none other than Monsieur Zachary Zidler. That was not, however, the name under which he had checked into the Hotel Magnificent. He had chosen instead to use an alias, keeping his real identity secret. (Perhaps it should give us pause for thought that he had been so bold as to tell the children his real name.)

Monsieur Petit looked flustered. "You can't mean Count Von Winkler? It looks a bit like him, yes, but he's one of our most esteemed guests. Been staying with us for three weeks now. I know because I gave permission for his dog to sleep in his room. Great big white monster of a creature it is too."

Inspector Balzac bent forward, cradling his head in his hands. "Just as I'd feared," he said, and sank back down into his chair.

"Would somebody mind telling me what is going on?" demanded Miss Goodwin. "These are my pupils. I insist on knowing what's happened to them!"

Inspector Balzac felt the sweat prickling on his forehead. The schoolteacher had a nasty habit of making him feel like he was the one under interrogation.

"It seems," he began cautiously, "that every year, somewhere in mainland Europe a group of schoolchildren go missing on this date. Each time, sightings have been reported of a man with a handlebar moustache and a large white dog."

"W-w-hat?" stammered Miss Goodwin. "But that's outrageous! Why have I never read about this in the papers?"

Inspector Balzac shifted nervously in his seat. "This kind of thing is always top secret. Our governments would never allow the press to print it. Think what it would do to tourism. Every parent in Europe would be up in arms."

Miss Goodwin paled, struck by a horrible thought. "Oh, my giddy aunt! *The parents!* I'm going to have to tell them."

The fear whistled up through her stomach like steam rising in a kettle.

"They'll annihilate me!" she wailed.

13

The Chateau Mistral

"There it is! Look! Crikey ... it's enor–mous!"

In the end it was Bruno who spotted the castle first. All the other children had been peering in the wrong direction. Now they jostled in their seats as they fought for a view of it.

"Where?"

"Let me see!"

"I can't see it!"

"It's right in front of you, dingbats," said Bruno. "Just look up!"

One by one, each child lifted his or her gaze to the mountain peak and fell silent. There, jutting out from the bare grey rock, was the most majestic castle any of them had ever seen. It loomed over them, a vast glittering structure that shone more brightly than the sun. The children gaped at the sight, awestruck by the scale of its architectural extravagance. The castle must have boasted at least a thousand archers' windows. Silken banners fluttered from its turrets. The domed roofs of its towers were painted a brilliant sky blue and seemed to reach right up into the clouds. Strange gargoyles, carved in the shapes of mythical monsters, leered down from the solid-gold gutters.

Whoever ruled Phartesia must be stinking rich to live in a palace like this, Bruno thought to himself.

The last bit of road leading up to the castle was steep and winding. The children held their breath as Monsieur Zidler slipped the car into first gear and began the ascent. There was danger on all sides. Smashed boulders were piled up to the left of them, evidence of recent rock falls. To their right was a crumbling cliff edge. One false move and they would all go plunging into the forest below. Unable to look, the children covered their eyes with their hands.

At last they heard the engine cut out as Monsieur Zidler brought the car to a halt near the summit of the mountain. The children tumbled out onto on the roadside. A cold wind howled in their ears.

"Wow," said Grace, pulling her blazer tight about her chest, "just look at this view! We're even higher than the birds."

It was true. Below them, a flock of starlings was flying in formation over the forest. Seen from above, they looked just like a shoal of fish progressing through a deep green river. As far as the eye could see there were no towns or cities,

97

just an occasional curl of wood smoke rising from the trees below.

The castle was surrounded by a wide moat. Bruno peered down at the rushing water, wondering how you were supposed to get across. There was no sign of a bridge. Suddenly he felt his blood run cold. A dozen black triangles were sticking up out of the water.

"Sharks!" he gasped, jumping back from the water's edge.

"So much better than a burglar alarm, don't you think?" said Monsieur Zidler, appearing beside him.

"Er, I guess so," replied Bruno a little nervously.

Monsieur Zidler reached into his pocket for a small tin whistle and gave a shrill two-note call. Almost at once there came a clank of heavy iron chains. Far above, a wooden drawbridge yawned open. So *that* was how you entered!

"Last one over is a piece of fish food!" called Xanadu, bounding across the polished oak planks. When he reached the halfway point, he performed a couple of cartwheels for good measure. Somehow, throughout this gymnastic display, his sunglasses remained stuck to his head. Not wanting to be left behind, the others rushed after him.

Monsieur Zidler brought up the rear with Trumpet, cane and tail swinging together in perfect time.

Once they had crossed the drawbridge and passed through the castle gates, the children found themselves in a vast courtyard, the walls of which were covered in mosaics depicting dancers, actors and musicians. Unsure what to do next, the children hovered nervously in the shadow of an enormous stone balcony.

"Don't be shy!" cried Monsieur Zidler, prodding them forward with his cane. "Step out into the light, where you can be seen."

Trumpet used her fleshy brown nose to help shepherd the children into the middle of the courtyard. Grace stayed close to Bruno's side as, from somewhere deep inside the castle, there came the sound of drumming. Bruno shivered with anticipation. In addition to the drumming, a strange droning could also be heard. And this drumming and droning was getting louder by the second. Soon it felt as if they were standing right inside the humming heart of a beehive.

The doors to the castle swung open and hundreds of moustachioed knights swarmed through. Their swords were drawn from their holsters and held tight to their chests. Their pompomed clogs lifted towards the sky as they goose-stepped round and round in a series of ever decreasing circles. Some of the knights' moustaches were so long that they trailed along the ground behind them. Bruno noticed that the more medals a knight had pinned to his chest, the more impressive seemed to be his moustache. The knights with the longest moustaches of all were not carrying swords, but instruments on which they played a bombastic military tune.

There was a terrific clash of cymbals and, as one, the knights stopped marching. They stomped their clogs together, then turned to face the centre of the courtyard. Bruno and Grace found themselves surrounded as Monsieur Zidler began to address the children in English.

"Pray silence for the national anthem of Phartesia!"

Clapping their hands over their hearts, the knights began to sing in lusty chorus:

"Et volcanicus erupticus exquisiticus,
In revengicus pharticus apocalypsum
Plus ferocicus que un turnipum
Childrenicus explodicus annulis."

"What does it mean?" Bruno whispered to Grace.

"I couldn't quite catch all of it," she admitted, "but it had something to do with an exploding volcano and a ferocious turnip."

Bruno was beginning to doubt the true extent of Grace's grasp of Phartesian.

"Cool song!" said Xanadu, bopping along. "Perhaps I'll cover it on my next album."

"Silence!" hissed Monsieur Zidler. "You will show respect to your hosts."

Bruno saw a shadow fall over the balcony from the room behind.

Trumpet barked, then raised a white paw in the air. A deafening shout went up around the courtyard as all the knights cried out, "Al halicus ye Duck di Phartesia!"

"Uh-oh," said Natasha, with a mocking glance at Grace. "Here comes the dreaded duck..."

14

The Biggest Moustache of All

The figure that flounced out onto the balcony did not have feathered wings, nor a yellow bill nor even webbed feet.

Instead, the children found themselves gazing up at a spindly little man in a cherry-coloured doublet and baby-pink tights. His head appeared rather too big for his body, for on it he wore an elaborate powdered wig. His skin was painted a deathly white, giving the impression that he had been carved from ice. His eyes were as small and black as raisins. His cheeks were stained with rouge, like two strawberries squashed into the face of a snowman.

"Doh!" Grace muttered, bashing her hand

against her forehead. "I'm such an idiot! Of course, he's the *Duke* of Phartesia!"

Bruno stared up at the duke, transfixed. Never had he seen such facial hair! The knights' moustaches were impressive, but the duke's was truly mesmerizing. It extended out like a looped line of handwriting across the sky, and on either side stood a trusty moustache-bearer, supporting the wispy ends on a polished gold tray.

The duke stepped up to the edge of the balcony and the trusty moustache-bearers shuffled forward with him. Gently, as if it were spun from silver thread, they draped the Royal Moustache over the edge of the balustrade.

The duke peered down at the children with his little raisin eyes. He spoke in heavily accented English, with a habit of stumbling over any word that began with an "f". (Curiously, this letter does not feature in Phartesian.)

"F-f-forgive me for asking, Zidler," he began, "but why, pray, have you brought this unfortunate bunch of windless wastrels here? I thought I'd been clear that this year I needed children with real talent."

Nervously, Monsieur Zidler smoothed his oil-slicked hair. He cleared his throat.

"I agree that they may look a little less than impressive, Your Majesty. But there's one boy the Trumpenhund sniffed out especially. I'm certain that I have here for you a true genius!"

The duke's voice dripped sarcasm like an oozing bag of rubbish. "Do you mean to say, Zidler, that you've actually f-f-found me a child capable of performing the starring role?"

Monsieur Zidler gleefully twiddled his moustache. Trumpet joyously wagged her tail. "Oh yes, Your Highness! My Trumpenhund is never wrong!"

The duke's mood changed in an instant.

He squealed with delight. "F-f-fabulous! Well, let's have a look at this genius! Such great talent deserves to be recognized!"

Each convinced that they were the genius in question, Humbert, Xanadu and Natasha were already barging their way to the front.

Bruno felt something wet nudging at the back of his legs. He turned to see the Trumpenhund pushing him forward with her big brown nose. Monsieur Zidler's smile was as bright as the spotlight now shining on Bruno.

"This is the boy!"

The duke wedged a monocle above one rouged cheek. He squinted down at Bruno, taking in his bushy eyebrows, sticky-out ears and unkempt hair.

"Surely you don't mean to suggest that this f-f-feral-looking f-f-foundling has what it takes to become a legend?"

Monsieur Zidler gave a helpless shrug. "It's hard to fathom, I know. But Trumpet's instincts are never wrong. There's no other explanation. The boy must be a genius."

This was news to Bruno. But what did it matter? If Monsieur Zidler was convinced he was a genius, he wasn't about to argue.

The duke's mouth twisted into a smile. "Well then," he simpered, "I'm sure we'll all be quite *blown away* by the boy's talent. But come, the children must be f-f-fatigued after their journey. We'll investigate their abilities f-f-further in the morning."

The duke clapped his hands. The trusty moustache-bearers rushed forward with their trays.

15

Stunkenstew

After the duke's speech, Monsieur Zidler showed the children up to a luxurious dormitory filled with four-poster beds. All the furniture was gilded with gold leaf and the carpet was as soft as a freshly mown lawn. There, in the grand sleeping quarters, a fierce battle was waged between excitement and exhaustion. At first it looked as if excitement would triumph: beds were bounced on, pillows were flung. But then eyelids began to droop, yawns proved contagious and before you could say, "Is that really Natasha snoring like a walrus?" exhaustion had won.

The children were woken at dawn by a familiar sing-song voice. "Wakey-wakey! Time to get up!"

For a split second Bruno thought he was back

on board *The Jolly Codger* with Grandpa Trevor and Chippy. Then he felt something wet rub against the soles of his feet. The Trumpenhund had stuck her nose under the duvet and was eagerly licking them. The events of the previous day came flooding back. Smiling to himself, Bruno sat up in bed. He was staying in a castle! In a beautiful country called Phartesia! Best of all, Monsieur Zidler had proclaimed him a genius!

Xanadu back-flipped out of the next bed.

"Did you actually sleep in those sunglasses?" asked Bruno, incredulous.

"You can laugh now," scoffed Xanadu, "but you won't be laughing when I whop your behind in the auditions!"

"We'll see about that," replied Bruno. "I was chosen especially, remember."

Chosen. What a lovely word that was.

At the other end of the room, Monsieur Zidler was pulling back the purple damask curtains. Sunlight filled the dormitory, illuminating the motes of dust. How blue the sky was up here above the clouds, thought Bruno. He glanced around at the others. Grace was yawning and rubbing her eyes. Humbert was stretching like a tomcat in his new satin pyjamas. Natasha was sitting up in bed brushing her long black hair. It suited her better down, thought Bruno. If only she would smile, she might almost look pretty.

"Time to get dressed," instructed Monsieur Zidler. "There are clean clothes on the ends of your beds. Can't have you looking scruffy for the auditions!"

Relishing the chance to wear something other than his nasty school uniform, Bruno dived straight into the pile of clothes. It seemed their new wardrobe consisted of a crisp white shirt, a cream silk waistcoat, black trousers and a black swallowtail jacket. Still a little on the old-fashioned side, but anything was better than itchy wool shorts.

"I'll be back in ten minutes to take you to breakfast," said Monsieur Zidler, and sauntered out of the room.

When he had slipped on the swallowtail jacket,

Bruno went to inspect himself in the mirror. His frizzy hair was still fuzzy. His sticky-out ears still stuck out. One bushy eyebrow was still bushier than the other. But, for once in his life, he felt smart.

Grace sidled up behind him, wearing exactly the same. She stiffened her arms, stuck out her toes and waddled around in a circle. "We look like a right pair of penguins," she moaned.

Bruno grinned at her in the mirror. He gave a clumsy bow and waved an imaginary cane in imitation of Monsieur Zidler. "I think we look sophisticated," he said. "What's wrong? Aren't you having fun?"

Grace shrugged. "I'm just not sure what we're doing here. Don't you think it's odd that no one's told us what we're actually auditioning *for*?"

Bruno threw up his hands, exasperated. "Where's your sense of adventure? We're here to become famous! Didn't you hear Monsieur Zidler? These knights can turn us into legends!"

"To tell you the truth, Bruno," confessed Grace, "I'm not really sure I want to be famous. Everybody knowing your business and writing mean things about you in the papers… I don't think I'd enjoy it."

Bruno looked at her as if she'd gone mad. How could anyone not want to be famous? Before he could respond, their conversation was interrupted by Monsieur Zidler returning to summon them to breakfast.

"Superstardom is hungry work," he warned, chivvying them all out of the room. "Make sure you eat up everything on your plates!"

Breakfast was served in a dining hall that was every bit as splendid as their bedroom. Though there were only seven of them (including Trumpet and Monsieur Zidler), the table was long enough to seat at least a hundred. The children were spaced out at intervals, which made it difficult to communicate without shouting. Monsieur Zidler sat at the head of the table with Trumpet at his right-hand side. The solid oak chairs were far too big for the children. Bruno's feet dangled down below his seat, way off the ground. Even the cutlery seemed large and unwieldy, cast as it was from solid silver and set with rubies and pearls. So much finery promised a feast of epic proportions.

Bruno's mouth watered at the thought of what the palace cooks might have prepared. Whatever it was, it had to be an improvement on Grandpa Trevor's burnt offerings. Perhaps there'd be piles of pancakes drenched in maple syrup, sizzling bacon, mountains of mango and melon or freshly baked loaves. The kinds of things you saw chefs whipping up on Saturday morning television.

A knight entered, bearing a steaming tureen. The ends of his moustache were covered with two little muslin nets. Bruno wrinkled his nose. Whatever breakfast was, it didn't smell like pancakes or freshly baked bread.

The knight lifted the lid, letting loose a silvery cloud of steam. Phewee! It smelt like sewers and skunks and mouldy old socks.

Down at the other end of the table, Humbert was pretending to retch. "Ugh. That smells disgusting!"

Ignoring him, Monsieur Zidler rattled his spoon against a crystal goblet. He stood up and spoke in a booming voice.

"This morning's breakfast is a splendid home-made Stunkenstew. The smell takes some time to get used to, but I can assure you it is quite delicious."

Bruno was determined to like everything about

Phartesia – even this foul-smelling concoction. Gingerly, he dipped in his spoon…

Monsieur Zidler was right. Despite the noxious smell, the stew really was good. In fact it was perhaps the tastiest thing Bruno had ever eaten. He tried another spoonful, then smiled encouragingly at Grace, who was seated ten spaces down to his left. He shouted so she could hear.

"It's really nice, I promise." But Grace had her own reasons to be suspicious. She raised her hand politely.

"Excuse me," she called down to Monsieur Zidler, "but could you please tell me exactly what's in this?"

Monsieur Zidler tapped his nose conspiratorially. "I'm afraid the recipe for Stunkenstew is a Phartesian state secret."

Grace continued to look anxious. "The thing is," she persisted, "I've got a few allergies. If I eat anything I'm not meant to, you might have to call for an ambulance."

Monsieur Zidler considered this possibility for a second. "I suppose it can't hurt to let a few little children in on the secret. Stunkenstew is a highly delicious blend of turnips, sardines, runner beans, corned beef, aniseed, oysters, white truffle and curdled cream cheese."

Choking on her own disgust, Natasha spat her stew back into her bowl. She summoned the knight with the silver tureen.

"You can't seriously expect me to eat this! Bring me something else, immediately – and don't be expecting a tip." The knight's face remained blank. Monsieur Zidler smiled apologetically.

"I'm afraid this is all there is. But you mustn't let the unusual ingredients put you off. Stunkenstew is considered quite a delicacy in these parts." He shot a sly smile at Natasha. "Perhaps your palette is simply not mature enough to appreciate such sophisticated fare."

Monsieur Zidler could not have chosen his words better. With a toss of her plait, Natasha plunged her spoon back into her stew.

"Mmmmm," she said, swallowing a mouthful with an exaggerated expression of pleasure. "Delicious."

The other children followed her example. What choice did they have? They hadn't eaten since the sandwiches in the car yesterday. In all the excitement of arriving at the castle, dinner had been forgotten, but now their stomachs ached with hunger. Soon they were all holding their noses and wolfing down big greedy mouthfuls.

As Bruno scraped the last morsel from his bowl, he felt a strange stirring in his tummy. Oh well. He shrugged. A bit of indigestion was normal, he supposed, what with the nerves and eating such rich food on an empty stomach.

Donnnnggg! The castle bells sounded the hour.

Monsieur Zidler's face was solemn. "Everybody follow me," he said, wiping his mouth delicately with a napkin and rising from his seat.

Bruno felt a rush of excitement. Now they would finally find out how they were going to become famous.

16

Behold the Ancient Phartling Hall

Deep inside the bowels of the castle, Monsieur Zidler's moustache cast snake-like shadows on the wall as he marched the children down a narrow, candlelit passageway lined with suits of armour. The corridor was only wide enough for one person to pass through at a time, so they walked in single file.

"Ouch! Careful!"

Bruno felt someone step down hard on the back of his heel. He turned to see Humbert scowling at him in the gloom.

"Hey, Stink Bomb! What was all that about yesterday? Why didn't you just tell the duke that

I'm the real genius? *A young man who threatens to move audiences to tears* – that was my last review in *Junior Fiddler's Monthly*."

Bruno was unimpressed. He rolled his eyes. "Since when has being good at the violin made anyone famous?"

"Er, that'd be apart from Paganini, Heifetz and Yehudi Menuhin, would it?" said Humbert, reeling off a list of names that meant nothing to Bruno.

"They're not famous," he dismissed. "I've never heard of them!"

"Dudes," said Xanadu, loafing up behind them, "I'm the one about to get a major record deal. Don't you think I might be the genius in question?"

Humbert spun round to give Xanadu a shove. Xanadu clutched at Bruno for support. The three boys went stumbling backwards into a suit of armour. Helmet and breastplate clattered to the floor together with a dozen other rusty pieces of metal.

"What did I say about squabbling?" Monsieur Zidler called back down the passageway. "A true star behaves with dignity and decorum!"

"Sorry, Monsieur Zidler," chimed all three boys in chorus.

"Now, come along. We mustn't keep His Royal Highness waiting."

A few minutes later, the group came to a halt outside a magnificent carved oak doorway.

"Behold the Ancient Phartling Hall!" announced Monsieur Zidler and flung back the doors.

The children gaped in amazement.

Even by the standards of the castle, this room was impressive: a vast underground theatre with circular walls hewn from the finest pink marble. At the far end was a stage draped with red velvet curtains. There were rows and rows of gilt-edged seats. Tiers of balconies reached up to an ornately painted ceiling, where cherubs blew gusts of wind across a starlit sky. In the centre of this ceiling hung an enormous chandelier, its crystal branches shimmering.

"Time I went and joined the duke," said Monsieur Zidler, ushering the children into the front row. "You sit here until we call you onto the stage."

Bruno turned to Grace, his brown eyes sparkling.

"What a cool place for an audition! It's like being inside a wedding cake."

But Grace wasn't listening. She was staring up

at an oil painting that hung between two marble pillars to one side of the stage. The painting was a life-sized portrait of a man in an old-fashioned dinner suit. An enigmatic smile played about the corners of his lips, and resting on his right shoulder was the mouth of a large brass horn. This horn looked a lot like a tuba, but Grace could see one crucial difference.

"What's so fascinating?" asked Bruno, following her gaze.

"There's something weird about that picture. Look closely and you'll see what I mean."

Bruno peered up at the painting. At first he noticed nothing out of the ordinary. Then he started with shock. Grace was right. There was something very strange indeed about the painting. The tube of the horn did not lead up to the man's mouth. Instead, it coiled around his body like a golden boa constrictor. If Bruno wasn't mistaken, it seemed to stop at his rear…

"Holy cow," whispered Bruno. "Is he playing that thing with his b-u-m?"

"That's what it looks like." Grace giggled. "Hey, what's that noise?"

All five children stopped talking and listened.

119

The same droning sound they had heard yesterday was now coming from the direction of the passageway outside the Phartling Hall.

The doors to the theatre swung open and hundreds of knights filed in. They were chanting again:

"Et volcanicus erupticus exquisiticus,
In revengicus pharticus apocalypsum
Plus ferocicus que un turnipum
Childrenicus explodicus annulis."

The chanting reached a frenzied crescendo as the knights took their seats in the balconies around the theatre. Then, suddenly, the chanting stopped. The Phartling Hall fell silent, and at that moment the room was plunged into darkness.

"Al halicus ye Duck di Phartesia!" roared the knights.

Bruno caught his breath. A single spotlight lit up the Royal Box, which hung above the right side of the stage. Caught in this circle of light was His Highness the Duke of Phartesia. Diamonds glinted on his doublet. He gave a royal wave. Rubies glittered on his fingers.

Barely visible in the shadows behind the duke were the trusty moustache-bearers and Monsieur Zidler. The duke clapped his hands. The trusty moustache-bearers shuffled forward and unfurled the Royal Moustache until it hung down over the stage like two giant wisps of cobweb.

For the benefit of the children seated in the front row, once again the duke spoke not in Phartesian, but in English.

"We are gathered here in the hope of f-f-finding a new star to light up this stage. Soon our f-f-five young guests will be called to perform. But f-f-first we should consider what is at stake."

He leant forward over the edge of the box to address his young visitors directly.

"F-f-fame…" The word slithered out from the duke's lips at the slow, leisurely pace of a serpent emerging from its basket. "F-f-fame and f-f-fortune beyond your wildest f-f-fantasies… F-f-for we Knights Trumplar take the natural talent lying dormant within an ordinary child and train it until every f-f-flaw has been eliminated. Then we allow it to explode like a f-f-firework into the world! Allow me to present Monsieur John Pujol…"

The duke pointed to the portrait that Bruno and

Grace had been sniggering at just a few minutes before.

"Born the son of a F-F-French baker, Pujol possessed a most remarkable ability. Can you guess what that was?"

The children shook their heads.

"He used his derrière to suck in air! Then blew it out again, in a f-f-fragrant f-f-fanfare!"

Bruno could not believe his sticky-out ears. Was the duke saying that John Pujol was a gifted musical farter? Why, that was his special talent, too!

The other children were rolling around in their seats.

"How brilliantly vulgar," jeered Natasha, tears pouring down her face.

"The man's insane!" scoffed Humbert and snorted with laughter.

"It's gotta be some sort of stand-up routine," Xandu dismissed, grinning.

Grace leant over towards Bruno with a smile. "Xanadu's right. This must be some sort of comedy act. I bet 'the duke' is just a hired entertainer in fancy dress."

Bruno frowned. "I don't see what's so funny. I can fart musically too, remember. Sounds to me like this Pujol guy had a genuine talent."

It was true that behind them the knights were not laughing either. They were listening to the duke in rapt silence.

"One day, as history records, a travelling knight spotted Pujol's potential and brought him to Phartesia. Here, he was trained to play an instrument whose melody is so dangerously beautiful, it has been banned in every other country in the world. What is this instrument, I hear you ask! Why, it is the king of all wind instruments! The f-f-fantastic, the f-f-fabulous … *phartlehorn*!"

The knights let out a patriotic roar of approval. The duke pressed on, now having to shout above them to be heard.

"The rich and the f-f-famous f-f-flocked to hear Pujol phartle. He gave secret performances in Paris, under the stage name Le Petomane, and soon he had riches beyond imagining."

Bruno's heart thumped in his chest. This was exactly the kind of opportunity he'd dreamt of all his life. If John Pujol could phartle his way to a fortune, why shouldn't he?

"But enough *talk* about music!" The duke clapped his hands. "The time has come for you to

123

hear with your own ears. Allow me to present my daughter, Her Royal Highness the Countess Strudel of Phartesia!"

"Al halicus ye Contessa Strudel di Phartesia!" roared the knights.

On stage, the velvet curtains drew back to reveal the most enchanting young woman Bruno had ever seen.

17

The Countess Strudel

Like her father, the countess had deep brown eyes.
The duke's eyes were muddy puddles; Strudel's
were midnight lakes in which you could happily
drown. Like her father, Strudel had startlingly
white skin. His was as creased and lined as
scrunched-up paper; hers was as luminous as
moonshine. Like her father, Strudel had blushing
pink cheeks. His were squashed strawberries; hers
were apples in the first flush of ripeness.

The countess acknowledged the knights'
applause with a demure curtsy. She was wearing a
cream silk dress shot through with golden thread.
Curls of flame-red hair licked at her porcelain
shoulders. Though she was in early adulthood,
Strudel spoke in a girlish lilting voice.

"What should I play, father?" she asked, looking up at the Royal Box.

The duke scratched his wig and thought for a moment.

"Something cheerful to welcome our new f-f-friends? Tchaikovsky's 'Sugar Plum F-f-fairy', perhaps?"

Strudel nodded. A low-ranking knight hurried onto the stage wheeling a large black case. Bruno watched as he swung back the lid to reveal a gleaming brass instrument, just like the one in the painting. In the light of the chandelier its elegant curves sparkled and shone.

"That must be a phartlehorn," whispered Grace.

"Beautiful!" sighed Bruno, his eyes fixed on the countess.

Strudel reached out to take the horn from the knight. She held it aloft like an enormous spiralling crown. Then, as elegantly as if she was slipping on a cashmere jumper, she brought it down over her head.

The duke smiled indulgently at his daughter. "F-f-feel f-f-free to begin..."

Intense concentration fell like a veil across Strudel's china-doll face. Then she began to play.

Bruno felt the hairs rise
on the back of his neck.
The sound was definitely
flatulent in origin. But,
oh, how lovely were
the notes! How powerful,
sweet and low. It was as if Bruno
heard them not with his ears,
but somewhere deep in the pit of
his stomach. The music permeated
every cell of his body, setting his
whole being humming to its tune.
A little shower of sparks fizzed
in his fingers and toes.

Two minutes into the
countess's performance,
Bruno found himself wiping the tears from his
eyes. Had he known the meaning of the word
"epiphany", that is exactly how he would have
described the feeling that struck him now. A
flash of certainty that changed the way he felt
about his life entirely. Listening to Strudel play
her phartlehorn was the first time Bruno had ever
felt sure of his true purpose. He wasn't a nobody.
He was a boy with an enormous natural talent!

127

He didn't care how crazy these knights seemed
with their moustaches, clogs and silly chanting.
It was fate that had brought him to Phartesia,
and he was ready to embrace his destiny.

All too soon, the countess's performance came
to an end. Along with the knights, the children
rose to their feet and cheered. Even the worldly
Natasha Oblonsky seemed to have been moved by
the music. For once her smile could be seen in her
eyes as well as her mouth. Only Humbert remained
seated, with his hands locked together in his lap, as
sour-faced as if he had swallowed vinegar.

"This isn't music," he hissed. "It's nothing but
hot air."

"You're just jealous," said Xanadu, who was
not, as it turned out, too big-headed to appreciate
genuine musical talent in others.

Strudel handed the phartlehorn back to the
knight. She swooped into another graceful curtsy,
then swept from the stage.

The Duke of Phartesia waited until the applause
had died down.

"Even as I speak, people are preparing to travel
here. People more f-f-famous than you can possibly
imagine. We Knights Trumplar have f-f-friends

in very high places. F-f-film stars! Politicians! Leaders of religion! All of them secret f-f-fans of phartistry! And you, my dear children, shall have the chance to phartle in f-f-front of them at a grand gala concert. One lucky solo phartiste will open the show. This afternoon, the f-f-five of you shall compete for that honour."

Bruno was listening to the duke with ears as wide as Trumpet's nostrils. Beside him, Grace was looking perplexed. This was not what she'd had in mind when she'd agreed to attend the auditions. Besides, there was something about the duke she did not quite trust. His enthusiasm whizzed about the hall like an out-of-control firework.

"Good luck, my f-f-fledgling phartistes," he called from the Royal Box. "And remember … do not waste a precious parp until your audition."

18

Agent Frogmarch's Briefing

Back at St Ermingarda's, Miss Goodwin stood marooned on the stage in the assembly hall, pleading for calm. Below her, a herd of hysterical parents were preparing to stampede. After a long night of police interviews, she and her remaining pupils had finally been allowed to fly home from France that morning. Taking off in bright sunshine, they had landed in the middle of a rain-soaked playing field. Unfortunately there had been no time to change out of her sundress. A parents' meeting had been scheduled for five minutes after her arrival.

"*Emergency! Emergency!*" squawked

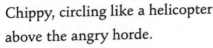

Chippy, circling like a helicopter above the angry horde.

Mrs Maldewicks opened her bright-red lips into a scream. "What have you done with my angel?"

"Just wait till my fans hear about this," screeched Shakti Messiah Brown. As befits a world-famous pop star, Xanadu's mother was the most outlandishly attired of all the parents. She wore an electric-blue jumpsuit embroidered with patches of neon-green lace. Her hair was shaved on one side and cut into a sharp, angular bob on the other.

"I'll – sue – you – for – every – measly – penny – of – your – salary," vowed Gregor Oblonsky. Each word the Russian billionaire spoke was punctuated with a puff of foul-smelling cigar smoke.

Grandpa Trevor threw his hands up in the air. "For heaven's sake," he shouted, "would you all keep calm and let Miss Goodwin speak? I, for one, would like to hear what's happened to my grandson."

"Here, here," cried Mrs Chalk, who was nursing a baby on her shoulder. "We should be working out how to help, not threatening lawsuits."

"Who cares what the stupid schoolteacher has to say," exclaimed Daria Oblonsky, a tall, thin woman in a long bearskin coat. "She's the one who lost our children!"

The end of her sentence was almost drowned out by the sound of heavy footsteps thundering down the corridor. The parents stopped shouting and looked at each other in confusion. They had not been expecting anyone else to join them. The doors to the assembly hall slammed open. Everyone gawped as a middle-aged woman in military uniform entered the room. The woman was as squat and square as a tank. Her hair was cut into the shape of a helmet and her boots were wet from the rain. Leaving a trail of muddy footprints in her wake, she stomped up to the stage and flashed an official-looking badge.

"Special Agent Frogmarch: Secret Society Branch of Her Majesty's Secret Service. I'll take over from here, Miss Goodwin."

The schoolteacher gladly surrendered the stage.

"Right, you lily-livered bunch of civilian cowards," the special agent bawled. "Shut up and sit down! Don't scrabble around for chairs! If your children can sit cross-legged on the floor, so can you!"

Agent Frogmarch's voice was as cold and deep

as an avalanche, and the threat that lurked beneath her glacial exterior was just as deadly. Terrified, the parents did as they were told. The hall was filled with the sound of knees clicking like un-oiled locks. Chippy fluttered down to perch on Grandpa Trevor's shoulder.

Agent Frogmarch waited until everybody was sitting quietly. She waved a manilla folder in the air. The words **TOP SECRET** were stamped across it in red ink.

"You are about to receive a briefing," she said. "This briefing contains highly classified state secrets. If even a drop of these secrets leaks out, I will personally hunt down the blabbermouth, and block the hole in their bucket with a hand grenade. Understand?"

Eager to prove that they could indeed keep their mouths shut, the parents nodded their reply.

"Good," said Agent Frogmarch. "Now that you've learnt to take orders, we can begin." She flipped open the folder. "My intelligence suggests that your children have fallen into the hands of an underground organization known as the Knights Trumplar."

The special agent cracked her knuckles. She smiled as if she was cracking the skull of an old enemy.

"The Knights Trumplar is an ancient secret society. Unfortunately, although we have our suspicions, we cannot say for certain in which country they are based. What we do know, however, is that this is their secret symbol..."

She flashed up a picture of a handlebar moustache.

"And this is their secret uniform..."

She flashed up a photograph of a man wearing a blue-and-white silk doublet and scarlet pompomed clogs.

"The origins of the Knights Trumplar are said to date back to the Crusades. Present members have two things in common. First, they're all stinking rich. Second, they share a fanatical love of *wind* instruments."

Readers who have been paying even the slightest bit of attention will be familiar with many of the state secrets contained in Agent Frogmarch's briefing. It was, however, all news to the parents.

"What's this got to do with our daughter?" whispered Daria Oblonsky.

Agent Frogmarch fixed Natasha's mother with an icy stare, and the Russian woman shrunk down inside her coat until only her eyes peeped out above the collar. It looked as though she was being eaten alive by the unfortunate bear whose skin she wore on her back. If only that were true, thought Agent Frogmarch, returning to her notes.

"Ever since mankind evolved from monkeys, we have loved music. At first we were happy to bash sticks on tree stumps. Soon we grew bored of our primitive banging and bonging, and our ears craved a more sophisticated variety of sounds to accompany our song. Over the centuries we have invented whole orchestras of instruments, many of which are still played today. These include, for example, the piccolo, the harpsichord, the xylophone and the bassoon. There is, however, one instrument known to our ancestors which has not been heard in public for more than a hundred years. Does anyone know what that instrument is?"

Silence.

Agent Frogmarch thrummed her fingers against her tattooed tricep. "The phartlehorn!"

None of the parents looked any the wiser.

"Allow me to enlighten you," bellowed the special agent. "A phartlehorn is an instrument designed to be played not with your mouth … but with your *backside!*"

There was a gasp from the audience. Agent Frogmarch's words lingered in the air like a bad smell.

"Preposterous!" scoffed Mr Maldewicks, his face every bit as sneering as his son's.

"Utter codswallop!" said Mr Oblonsky, whose bearskin coat was even bigger than his wife's.

"I'm a classically trained musician," boasted Shakti Messiah Brown, "and I've never heard of this ridiculous instrument!"

Mr Messiah Brown arched his over-plucked eyebrows, then languidly crossed his legs. "To be fair, dearie, you can't actually *play* an instrument.

As I recall, on your last album you didn't even sing."

"Oh shut up," snapped his wife. "Or I'll cut your allowance."

Only Grandpa Trevor did not join in the chorus of disbelief. He had a sinking feeling that Agent Frogmarch was telling the truth. Could his grandson's talent for musical farting really be a coincidence? It seemed unlikely.

Mr Chalk politely raised his hand. He'd come straight from work and was still in his dustman's overalls.

"Perhaps, Agent Frogmarch, you could show us a phartlehorn so we could see for ourselves?"

"Impossible," she said dismissively. "Phartistry has been outlawed for well over a century. Banned as an affront to public decency! The Treaty Against Phartistry was signed by President Abraham Lincoln, Emperor Napoleon III and Queen Victoria herself!"

The icy glint in Agent Frogmarch's eyes had now turned to fire. The audience could hear the awe in her voice as she told of the destruction that had been wrought upon phartistry.

"That was the summer they called the Apocalypse of the Phart. Public performances of phartistry were banned. Known Knights Trumplar were chased from every civilized country. Every last brass phartlehorn was melted down for scrap and replaced in orchestras by that far inferior instrument, the tuba." She sighed. "All that we have left is a rare recording seized from a Russian aristocrat fleeing the Revolution. Listen very carefully, I will play this only once."

The special agent reached down under the lectern and pulled out a bulletproof suitcase, made from solid steel and secured with a large combination padlock. Her stubby fingers fumbled to unscramble the code. Then, finally, she flipped open the suitcase. Inside lay an old-fashioned gramophone on which rested a battered record.

"'Air on the G String' by Johann Sebastian Bach is perhaps the most famous piece of music ever written for the phartlehorn."

Gently, the special agent coaxed the needle into the groove. A faint crackle filled the air, like the breeze that comes before a storm. Then the gramophone burst into song.

Grandpa Trevor felt a wave of shock break over his body. He knew the piece, of course, but on all previous occasions he'd heard it played on the violin. Now he listened in reverie to the most startling music his ears had ever encountered. The notes flowing out of the gramophone were rich and low, with a mournful resonance that made the three hairs on his head bristle in delight.

As if the heavens were trying to compete, rain began to thrash against the roof. Thunder broke high in the clouds above. But nothing Mother Nature had to offer could compare with the unworldly music of the phartlehorn. To hear such music, such unequalled music, was almost more pleasure than Grandpa Trevor could bear.

All too soon, the recording came to an end. Grandpa Trevor felt a flush of guilt. If only he'd taken Bruno's gift more seriously.

Not everyone in the assembly hall had been so moved.

"Thanks for the cultural lecture," sniffed Shakti Messiah Brown. "But what has this got to do with my missing son?"

"Listen up, you over-hyped karaoke singer," barked Agent Frogmarch, "you might just learn something. Ever since phartistry was first outlawed, each spring the Knights Trumplar have marked the anniversary of their exile by kidnapping a group of schoolchildren. They do this, it is thought, in revenge for the humiliations they have suffered. This is the first time that British citizens have been taken. It is therefore the first time the crime has fallen under my jurisdiction. Something I am sure the Knights Trumplar will come to regret. But the point I am trying to make is this: my initial investigations have revealed that among the victims there is always one child who is an unusually talented trumper."

Her eyes roved around the assembly hall like laser beams, and she allowed them to rest on each parent in turn.

"Would anyone like to confess to such a talent in their child?"

Gregor and Daria Oblonsky sunk even further down inside their coats. Mr and Mrs Maldewicks stared up at the ceiling. The Chalks looked at each other in confusion. The Messiah Browns were too busy arguing to answer.

"Pop goes the stinker! Pop goes the stinker!"

declared Chippy, flapping her wings.

Grandpa Trevor slowly raised his hand. "My grandson Bruno," he announced proudly, "is perhaps the most prodigious parper the world has ever seen."

The other parents glared. So it was this elderly seaman's fault that their children had been kidnapped! How dare such a penniless nobody send his grandson to the same school as their precious progeny?

Mr Oblonsky turned to Grandpa Trevor and blew out a ring of smoke. It hung like a noose in the air. "Just you wait till Agent Frogmarch finds that boy. Why, I'll make him wish he'd never been rescued."

Mrs Chalk looked suddenly hopeful. "Agent Frogmarch," she said, "you will find our children, won't you? They did rescue the other missing children ... didn't they?"

A shadow fell across the craggy plains of Agent Frogmarch's face. She snapped shut her bulletproof suitcase, then descended from the stage. "It is my sad duty to report that in fact none of these children have ever been found." She paused in the doorway. "Actually, that's not *entirely* true. We have found bits of them. But we've never found a whole one."

The assembly hall doors banged shut behind her.

Grandpa Trevor stepped out through the St Ermingarda's school gates and into a blaze of flash photography. Paparazzi: all fighting for a shot of the world-famous pop diva Shakti Messiah Brown in her hour of personal tragedy. The glossy magazines would pay thousands for a picture.

Gregor Oblonsky stormed into the scrum of reporters. He grabbed an unsuspecting cameraman by his shirt collar and wrenched him out from the crowd. The cameraman's eyes bulged in fear.

"You want an exclusive?" demanded the billionaire. "Then film this, you pathetic little parasite!"

Terrified, the cameraman pressed record.

"This is a message to my daughter's kidnapper," puffed Gregor Oblonsky. "I don't give a boiled beetroot about your musical mania. This year you have picked the wrong parent to mess with. To anyone who can help bring about the safe return of my beloved Natasha, I offer five million pounds. To anyone who hurts a hair on her head, I promise a lifetime of punishment and pain."

With that, the Russian oil baron crunched the end of his cigar beneath his boot and stomped off towards his chauffeur.

"Gregor," bayed the photographers, knowing it would annoy him if they used his first name. "Tell us more about your missing daughter. Daria, do you have any reason to believe Natasha is still alive?"

But it was too late. The Oblonskys were already gliding away in their black Phantom Rolls Royce.

Now the other parents jostled to make their own appeals to camera. As you know, St Ermingarda's was a highly exclusive establishment. The parents of Bruno's classmates were not short of cash to splash on kidnapped children. Soon the reward fund had topped ten million pounds.

Grandpa Trevor stood alone on the pavement. In his rush to get to the meeting he had forgotten his umbrella. Raindrops trickled down his bald head, mingling with the tears that streaked his cheeks. Chippy was perched on a nearby lamp post, her feathers wet and bedraggled.

A little way off, Mrs Chalk was rocking her baby to sleep under the shelter of its waterproof pushchair cover. Noticing the old man's distress, she waggled her large rainbow-striped umbrella, motioning for him to step in out of the wet.

"No fun being here on your own, is it?" she said with a kindly smile. "My husband's had to go back to work. Why don't you and the parrot come home with Georgie and me? I'll make up the sofa bed and warm through a bit of chicken soup. People should stick together at a time like this."

Grandpa Trevor didn't want to intrude, but the thought of another night alone on a cold and leaky boat without Bruno was hard to face.

"Thank you," he said. "That's very kind."

"Home is where the heart is," warbled Chippy, swooping down to join them. "Home is where the heart is."

"Not without Bruno it's not," said Grandpa Trevor with a sigh.

19
Phartesia's Next Top Trumper

The children stood in a line at the back of the stage, dressed in their matching black-and-white suits. Lunch had been another helping of Stunkenstew. By now the side effects of a traditional Phartesian diet were becoming all too apparent. The faint stirring that Bruno had felt at breakfast had morphed into a violent rumbling. He could hear his stomach gurgling like an over-excited jacuzzi, and the waistband of his trousers had grown uncomfortably tight.

Bruno looked anxiously at the other children. It seemed he wasn't the only one experiencing these symptoms.

"Your belly's as big as a football!" jeered Humbert and poked Natasha in the tummy.

"Well, so's yours," she said, poking him right back.

Grace was looking a little queasy.

"Are you OK?" whispered Bruno.

She shook her head. "I feel ridiculous."

"I thought you said you liked the idea of musical parping?"

"I do," she replied defensively. "I just wasn't planning on making a *career* out of it."

Bruno sighed and turned away. There was just no pleasing some people. Up in the Royal Box, the countess was taking a seat between her father and Monsieur Zidler. The thought of having to audition in front of such a talented musician made Bruno panic. After all those years spent practising in his bathroom, his whole future now rested on this one performance.

The duke rose to his feet. "I can sense you are all close to *bursting* with nerves... Well, f-f-fear not. While there can be only one solo phartiste, you shall all have the chance to give an *explosive* performance at the concert!"

The knights, who usually remained so expressionless, began to snigger. What was it they found so amusing? Bruno wondered.

The duke waited for the noise to die down. "At today's audition you shall not be required to play a phartlehorn. Instead you must simply demonstrate the f-f-force of your personal instrument."

Natasha tapped her foot, pouting. When this failed to provoke any response, she reluctantly raised her hand.

"Yes, what is it?" snapped the duke.

"Do you mean, Your Highness, that you want us to –" she looked as if she had swigged from a carton of sour milk "– fart?"

The duke let out a scandalized gasp. "*That* is not a word we like to use here in Phartesia," he sniffed. "Vulgar people may use that term. I prefer to refer to the exquisite emanations of the human derrière as *phartling*."

"But doesn't it stink?" asked Humbert, disgusted.

"Only an uncultured imbecile would f-f-feel that way," said the duke witheringly. Bruno Pockley, as you were the one the Trumpenhund f-f-first sniffed out, we'll save your audition till last. Natasha, since you seem so confident in speaking up, perhaps you'd like to begin."

Natasha paled.

"Just express everything you feel welling up inside," encouraged the countess in her gentle, lilting voice.

"On the count of three." The duke beat time with a baton. "One … two … three!"

Natasha pursed her mouth, then bent into an elegant plié. *Wheeeshhh!* The air sailed out of her in a high-pitched wail then pinged around the marble walls of the theatre, tinkling against the crystal baubles of the chandelier. It smelt sharp, like swimming pools, and strangely metallic, as if she had been sucking on money.

"Bravo," cried the duke, "a most excellent way to commence!"

"What an original style!" praised his daughter.

Monsieur Zidler put a tick by Natasha's name in his notes.

"A clear contender for the solo phartiste," proclaimed the duke. "Now, who's next?"

Humbert pushed his way to the front. "Forget these amateurs," he shouted up at the Royal Box. "Wait till you hear what a true musical prodigy has to offer."

Humbert assumed the position. The duke swept down with his baton. The knights held their breath.

A low hiss, like a saucepan boiling over, rattled around the theatre. After a while the hiss became a reedy warble, as if someone was gently blowing over a milk bottle. There was a faint smell of sulphur in the air.

Monsieur Zidler, the duke and his daughter looked unimpressed.

"Hardly what I'd call a natural talent," said the countess. "Whatever were you thinking, Monsieur Zidler?"

"Next!" screeched the duke.

Humbert clenched his fists. "You cannot be serious! That was just a warm-up! It's not fair! I was just tuning my instrument!"

"A total disgrace!" pronounced Monsieur Zidler.

Humbert stormed off the stage.

Xanadu volunteered to take his turn next. The duke leant forward in his seat as he strutted across the stage. Here was a child who demanded to be looked at.

"Everybody Get Down!" cried Xanadu. Bruno looked on in amazement as the child star broke into an elaborate body-popping routine. He kinked his neck from side to side like a cobra. He tucked himself up into a ball and spun round on the floor.

He arched his back into a bridge. He jumped up and did the splits. Then, finally, he let rip. A three-tone gospel guff sang out through the hall.

The audience went wild. There was dancing in the aisles. The knights' moustaches wiggled and jiggled to the rhythmic reverberations. Xanadu sprang into a celebratory Brazilian Bonk Flip.

Bruno felt another surge of nerves, and something which might well have been jealousy. The competition was proving tougher than he'd expected.

"I think this boy could be the future of phartistry!" exclaimed the countess.

"My, oh my!" The duke whistled. "I do f-f-feel sorry for whoever's next. Who is it? Ah yes, Grace Chalk."

Bruno watched his friend march to the front of the stage. How small she looked, alone in the spotlight. And yet her face was set into an expression of pure determination. Grace might not like the idea of becoming a famous phartiste. But she sure as heck didn't want to be beaten by Natasha or Xanadu.

At the duke's count, Grace focused her sights on victory and blew out as hard as she could.

Boom! Boom! Boom!

The force of the explosion took everybody by
surprise. The audience gasped as Grace stumbled
backwards. Bruno looked on in horror as she lay
motionless on the floor. Then she opened her eyes
and burst out laughing.

"That was fun!" she exclaimed.

Monsieur Zidler, the duke and his daughter,
and two hundred knights leapt to their feet in
a standing ovation.

"Such a tiny girl! With such a powerful instrument!" the countess cried.

"Our new solo phartiste!" proclaimed the duke. "Surely no one can better that!"

Monsieur Zidler turned to the duke with a fawning smile. "Aren't you forgetting something, Your Highness? We still have to hear from Bruno."

The duke frowned. "Very well," he said. "I suppose we must give the boy a chance."

Bruno stepped to the front of the stage. Two hundred knights stared up at him. The sight of all those bristling moustaches chilled him to the bone. So this was what stage fright felt like. A sickening panic that left your head reeling and your lungs gasping for air. Bruno closed his eyes and tried to imagine he was back in the dank bathroom of *The Jolly Codger*.

The duke counted to three. Bruno sucked in his tummy muscles, then breathed out as hard as he could.

Nothing.

He squeezed harder.

Still nothing.

He squeezed harder still.

152

But it was no use. Not a whiff of a whistle, not a peep of a parp. The knights began to jeer. Bruno squeezed until his face was crimson. He squeezed until his eyes were pricked with tears. At last he felt the air start to move inside him. Squelch followed raspberry followed squelch. It sounded like the death throes of an aged hippopotamus. A stench, as stagnant as old flower water left to fester in the vase, skulked down from the stage.

"Eewk," squealed the duke. "How deliciously disgusting!"

"But not what I'd call an impressive noise," said the countess. "All in all a great disappointment! Zidler, that dog of yours must have a blocked nose. This boy will never make a solo phartiste."

Monsieur Zidler looked sheepishly down at the floor. What could he say? The boy was an utter let-down.

Bruno was furious with himself. He'd blown his one chance to impress. Or rather he hadn't. That was the problem.

The duke and his daughter huddled together, whispering. It took less than twenty seconds for them to reach a decision. The duke rose to his feet.

"Phartesia's next top trumper shall be…" The

153

knights were on the edge of their seats. "Grace Chalk!"

The applause from the theatre was thunderous. Over and over, the knights chanted Grace's name. She responded with a shy smile.

Bruno felt sick with envy. It was so unfair. Grace didn't even want to be famous. It should have been his name they were chanting, not hers. The duke waved his baton for quiet.

"Natasha and Xanadu shall also receive prominent parts in the concert. Over the next two days I shall personally supervise the tuition of the talented trumpers. Everything I know about phartistry I shall teach you."

The Countess Strudel pointed at Humbert and Bruno. "The two remedial parpers will receive tuition from me."

Bruno felt a small wave of relief. There was at least a glimmer of silver lining poking out from beneath the dark clouds of his disgrace.

20
A Spot of Telly

While the duke was delighted with how the auditions had gone, he was nonetheless exhausted by the day's excitements. He retired to the Royal Chamber at sunset, ordering the children to have an early night. As always, the trusty moustache-bearers accompanied him to his dressing table. There they set the Royal Moustache in heated curlers before leaving their master alone with his thoughts.

As he sat in front of the mirror and wiped off his make-up, the duke reflected on the emotional rollercoaster of the past few weeks. The strain was clearly visible on his face. Beneath the heavy white powder, his eye sockets were dark and his skin was threaded with crimson veins. All those nights he'd lain awake worrying that, this year, Monsieur Zidler might fail to find any children talented enough to set the stage alight at the annual concert. Now, here they were with the most exciting line-up they'd had in decades. He should have had more faith in the man. It was not as though Zachary Zidler had ever let him down before.

The duke slipped on his monogrammed dressing gown and clambered into bed to watch a bit of telly. He flicked lazily between channels, finally settling on the BBC News round-up. There was nothing that he enjoyed more at the end of the day than a large helping of other people's misery. Tonight's bulletin did not disappoint. First up was a report on a high-street bank that had just gone bust. Thousands of people were going to be forced to sell their homes. So what? thought the duke. The world would always need poor people. How else were rich people supposed to find servants?

Next, the screen was filled with the image of a famous pop star sobbing into a microphone. The duke turned the volume up. Now this looked interesting...

"For more on the mystery of the missing English schoolchildren," announced the presenter, "we are returning to St Ermingarda's School for Exemplary Young People, where earlier today international singing sensation Shakti Messiah Brown made this emotional statement to the press."

Shakti Messiah Brown looked up into the camera like a wounded deer. Propped against his pile of silken pillows, the duke felt uncomfortably like she was fluttering her eyelashes directly at him.

"I would like to express gratitude to the police officers who are searching so tirelessly for our missing children," she said. "But most importantly, I would like to make an appeal to my fans. Help me to find my Xanadu and I will give you front-row tickets and backstage passes to all my concerts, plus signed T-shirts and limited-edition posters."

157

This news was met with a collective gasp from the press. Tickets to Shakti's concerts were like gold dust. Her fans would stop at nothing to get their hands on them.

The screen was filled with images of Xanadu, set to a compilation of his mother's most tear-jerking ballads. It began with a picture of her picking him up from the orphanage in Cambodia. Here he was modelling his first pair of sunglasses and sucking on his award for Most Talented Baby in Britain. The video ended with a clip from his TV show and a number to call with information.

The duke sat bolt upright in his bed. His blood ran cold in his veins. This was the boy who had performed so confidently at the auditions that afternoon! Xanadu was the son of a famous pop star? He'd even had his own TV show? Whatever had Monsieur Zidler been thinking of, kidnapping *him*?

Furious, he clanged the bell for his butler. "Jobsworth!" he screeched. "Summon my moustache-bearers and the Grand Council of the Knights Trumplar! Have Monsieur Zidler escorted to the Council Chamber!"

"Certainly, Your Highness," said Jobsworth,

who had appeared, as if by magic, at his master's bedside. "Consider it done."

The duke was not the only one watching the BBC News broadcast. In a small terraced house in an unremarkable corner of South London, Grandpa Trevor and the Chalks also had their television on. As they listened to the other parents promising eye-wateringly large amounts of ransom, they felt helpless and inadequate. What did they have to offer in exchange for the safe return of their loved ones, save everlasting gratitude? Somehow they doubted the kidnappers would be interested in that.

On any other evening the living room of the Chalk household would be a hive of activity. Mrs Chalk was studying to become a legal secretary at night school. She and Grace would do their homework together at the table, while baby George played beneath it and Mr Chalk whipped up something nice for dinner. Tonight the atmosphere was far more sombre. The baby had been put to bed early, and Grandpa Trevor and the Chalks were slouched in a row on the sofa, bowls of chicken soup lying untouched on their laps.

"Do you think they're being mistreated?" asked

Mr Chalk, half-heartedly offering out a round of toast.

"Of course they're being mistreated," sniffed Mrs Chalk. "They've been kidnapped."

Grandpa Trevor tried to remain positive. "Perhaps they're enjoying themselves. I know I'd have loved the chance to learn a musical instrument at their age."

"Doh, ray, me," sang Chippy from her perch on the back of the sofa.

Mr and Mrs Chalk looked at the old man with sympathy. It was their guess that, like them, he'd not had many opportunities in life.

"Make your own luck, that's what I'm always telling Grace," said Mrs Chalk, blowing her nose into a handkerchief. "We can't just sit around here doing nothing. There must be some way we can help."

"Why don't we revisit the scene of the crime?" suggested Grandpa Trevor. "Have a hunt for clues?"

"Go to France?" said Mrs Chalk. "But how would we get there? We don't have any money for flights or train tickets, and we don't even own a car."

The three of them thought for a while. For

a brief moment, Grandpa Trevor considered unmooring *The Jolly Codger* and motoring her across the Channel. But he had to admit that the boat was full of leaks and would doubtless sink before they'd even reached Greenwich.

"I know!" cried Mr Chalk. "I could drive the rubbish truck! It might take a while, but she's a reliable old gal, and we'll get there in the end."

"Take the rubbish truck?" exclaimed Mrs Chalk. "Wouldn't that be illegal?"

Her husband was already changing into his uniform. "Come on, we can drop the baby off with your sister on the way to the depot."

Grandpa Trevor heaved himself up from the sofa. He reached out a hand to Mrs Chalk. "What do you say, Penny? I'm game if you are."

"Nothing ventured, nothing gained!" squawked Chippy. "Nothing ventured, nothing gained!"

Penelope Chalk jumped to her feet. Her face was set with an expression of quiet determination that will not be unfamiliar to those of us who have already met her daughter.

"I say those Knights Trumplar will rue the day they ever took my daughter…"

161

*   *   *

"Order! Order!" The Duke of Phartesia smashed down his ivory gavel. "I will have silence in the Council Chamber!"

The ten robed knights around the table fell quiet. What could be so important that they'd been summoned from their chambers at this late hour? Why was Monsieur Zidler standing shackled in the dock?

"Gentlemen of the Grand Council of the Knights Trumplar," continued the duke, "it seems we have a crisis on our hands!"

The knights nervously twiddled their moustaches. A crisis did not sound good.

The duke pointed at Monsieur Zidler. "It has come to my attention that this imbecile has managed to kidnap the son of a world-famous pop diva, the daughter of a Russian billionaire and goodness knows who else."

A ripple of shock ran round the council. The duke picked up a leather-bound book from the table. He wedged in his monocle and thumbed through until he had found what he was looking for.

"Rule number one of the Trumper Talent Scout's Code clearly states: *Lo, though he or she may let*

162

rip the most magnificent of parps, any child whose disappearance may create unusual public attention is not to be taken for training in phartistry." The duke snapped the book shut. "As I understand it, this Xanadu Messiah Brown has even had his own TV show! How could you have been so *stupid*? Explain yourself at once, man!"

Monsieur Zidler's expertly oiled moustache quivered in fear. "It was just a m-m-mistake, Your Excellency," he stammered. "The boy Trumpet sniffed out looked like a peasant. How was I supposed to know he was at school with a pop star's son?"

"Just a mistake?" squeaked the duke. "They were staying at the Hotel Magnificent! Of course they couldn't have been peasants! You do realize, do you not, that your 'mistake' has put the national security of Phartesia at risk! These parents are offering a ten-million-pound reward. That's not a temptation for anyone as rich as ourselves, of course, but this Shakti Messiah Brown has promised rare tickets to her concerts, and signed T-shirts. Very soon we'll have a whole bunch of bounty hunters traipsing about our kingdom. What do you have to say about that, hmm?"

Monsieur Zidler said nothing. The Duke of Phartesia looked at him with disdain. Everything about the Trumper Talent Scout stank of guilt. Once more the duke banged down his ivory gavel.

"Zachary Zephaniah Zidler, you have broken our most important law. Thus you must suffer the ultimate punishment. Guards, take him to the dungeons. I shall decide *exactly* how to dispose of him tomorrow!"

21
All that Glitters Is Not Gold

The children were woken at dawn. On this, their second morning at the castle, it was not Monsieur Zidler who came to rouse them, but the duke himself. He was accompanied by his two trusty moustache-bearers and his daughter. Strudel pulled back the curtains and stood with her back to the view. Sunlight streamed in behind her, lighting up her flowing blue robes and flame-red hair, causing her to glow like a figure in a stained-glass window.

Bruno blinked open his eyes, dazzled by the sight. The countess's expression was kind and almost maternal. The duke, on the other hand, looked as if he had recently swallowed poison.

What could have happened, Bruno wondered, to put him in such a bad temper?

A bony white finger pointed at Grace, Natasha and Xanadu.

"The three of you, meet me in the Phartling Hall straight after you've f-f-finished breakfast. You managed to impress me yesterday, but there's a lot of work to do before the concert."

The duke took a long look at Xanadu. "And you, boy," he said stabbing at the air with his finger, "had better go off with a bang!"

Xanadu's mouth flapped open and shut in confusion. "W-w-what did I do wrong?"

The countess gave her father a warning look. "Father! The children are here as our guests!" She turned to Xanadu with an apologetic smile. "Please forgive the duke. He can be a terrible grump in the mornings, but he's a sweetie really. What he means is that he's sure you'll bring the house down."

Bruno was surprised to see that the duke, who had been scowling furiously, was now pink with embarrassment.

"Yes, yes," he gushed, rushing over to Xanadu, "that's exactly what I meant. Do please f-f-forgive me."

The moustache-bearers struggled to reverse quickly enough as the duke then made a hasty retreat from the room.

While the other children began scrabbling into their uniforms, the countess turned her attention to Humbert and Bruno.

"I'll be waiting for you up in my music room," she said in her honey-sweet voice. "Just ask any knight to show you the way."

Half an hour later, Humbert and Bruno were sitting on either side of the countess at her grand piano. The music room was located at the top of the south turret. It was hexagonal in shape, with tapestries covering the walls and windows that looked out over the forest.

Bruno breathed in the scent of roses and jasmine that wafted from the countess's long red tresses. He squirmed in his seat, worried that his own hair might be starting to smell a little fusty. Without Grandpa Trevor there to remind him, it had somehow slipped his mind to wash it. To make matters worse, a large stain of Stunkenstew had appeared on his waistcoat. How was it that he always managed to look such a mess? Humbert was as clean as a surgeon's scalpel.

The countess tossed back her hair. "I'm afraid we have a long day ahead. But by the end, I'm sure we'll have you phartling like nightingales. Now, let's begin with some theory."

Humbert leant back in his chair and yawned theatrically. "I doubt there's anything you can teach me. I've already passed my grade eight with distinction."

Bruno kicked himself. If only he'd paid more attention in music class. Yet the countess seemed strangely unimpressed. She let out a long tinkling laugh.

"I think you'll find, Humbert, that the phartlehorn is quite different from any instrument you've played before. Now then, can either of you tell me where a phartle comes from? Perhaps your mothers might have explained?"

Bruno searched his brain for an answer, but to his dismay he found he didn't have a clue. "I don't have a mum any more," he said forlornly.

Humbert rolled his eyes. "You should count yourself lucky. I've got a mother and I wish I didn't. All she does is nag, nag, nag. 'Humbert, have you done this? Humbert, have you done that?'"

The countess spun round to face him. "Humbert! You mustn't say such a thing! You wouldn't be here without her!" She took Bruno's hands in hers. "I don't have a mother either. Mine died when I was just a baby. So you see we have something in common."

Bruno was dumbstruck. Countess Strudel was so beautiful and so talented, and yet here she was confiding in him as if he was a friend and equal. He stared down at their joined hands in wonder. Then, noticing the dirt beneath his nails, he quickly pulled his own hands away.

The countess produced a pencil and a pad of paper and Bruno watched in awe as her fingers darted across the page, conjuring an aeroplane in delicate grey strokes. When it was finished, she blew on the drawing to remove the little shavings of rubber. The countess looked like a fairy blowing moon dust over a meadow, thought Bruno.
But what did all this drawing have to do with phartling?

"Have you heard the sound a plane makes when it's flying?" asked the countess.

Bruno recalled the roar of the St Ermingarda's school jet and nodded.

Humbert stared out of the window, determined not to learn anything.

"Well, just as a plane converts fuel into a loud screech of air, so your body creates a phartle by converting undigested food into gas."

Mesmerized, Bruno watched the countess flip over the page and draw another picture on her pad.

"Phartles are created by the squillions of hungry bacteria that live inside your tummy. As they gorge their way through your guts they let off a constant flurry of little phartles of their own. Just imagine it, hundreds of microscopic bacteria popping off inside you all day long."

It was almost like magic, thought Bruno, how one moment the paper was blank and the next it was alive with teeming creatures. Even more thrilling was the thought of all those bacteria trumping away in his tummy.

"There's nothing like that living inside *my* stomach," dismissed Humbert. "I wouldn't allow it. I'd find some way to kill them."

The countess looked at him with pity in her eyes. "I'm afraid the body is a universe beyond our knowing. And don't believe anyone who tells you they don't phartle. If that were true, they'd be as dead as a Christmas goose."

Was it really true that everyone trumped that much? wondered Bruno. Even presidents or the Pope? He found it hard to believe.

Strudel not so much walked as floated across to the other side of the room, where she flung open the doors of a large mahogany cabinet. Bruno caught his breath. Three magnificent phartlehorns gleamed in the darkness. "Come and help yourselves," she said.

"Yeeeeessssssss!" The two boys charged towards the cupboard.

From the moment he had first heard the countess play, Bruno had been desperate to have a go on a phartlehorn. Just as he was about to lift out the shiniest of the three instruments, he felt it snatched from his grasp.

"Bad luck," said Humbert with a smirk, hoisting the horn up and over his head. "This one's mine."

Bruno tried to hide his disappointment as the countess took down a rather less grand phartlehorn and helped him to position it correctly on his shoulder.

"Don't tell Humbert," she whispered conspiratorially, "but this is a far superior instrument. All that glitters is not gold, remember."

Just how true those words were, Bruno had yet to discover.

The hours that followed were some of the happiest Bruno had ever known. The horn was heavier than he had expected, but he soon learnt how to balance it so that the weight was dispersed evenly about his body. The countess was a kind and patient teacher. She had a way of explaining things that Bruno found easy to understand. They began with simple scales then progressed to chords and arpeggios.

Without all the knights watching him, Bruno's natural talent for trumping quickly returned. By the time they broke for lunch, he was happily phartling out the opening bars of a sonata by Beethoven. The phartlehorn amplified his parps splendidly, making them sound more prodigious than ever.

Humbert, however, was struggling. Try as he might, he simply couldn't phartle in tune. When he was meant to be phartling quietly, the noise boomed out of him. When he was meant to be phartling loudly, barely a whisper could be heard. By teatime, Humbert could take it no more.

"This is a stupid instrument!" he cried, chucking the phartlehorn down onto the flagstone floor. It landed with an enormous clatter.

"Oh dear, oh dear," said the countess. "I think you'd better sit this next piece out. Bruno and I are going to try a little Mozart."

"It's not fair!" shouted Humbert. "Bruno doesn't even know who Mozart is! *I'm* the musician! He's just a stupid nobody!"

The countess rolled her eyes as Humbert stomped off into a corner. "I'll let you in on a little secret," she whispered to Bruno. "Very few people know the real Mozart. He was an amazing composer, but he was also a true connoisseur of phartistry. There's one line of his I always remember, from a letter to his mother: *Yesterday, we heard the king of farts. It smelled as sweet as honey tarts. Don't you think that's lovely?*"

173

"It's the most beautiful thing I ever heard," replied Bruno, bewitched.

Strudel sat down at the piano and flicked through a book of music. *"The Magic Phartlehorn* was Mozart's masterpiece," she told Bruno. "Although, of course, that's not the name most people know it by. This is the piece with which the solo phartiste traditionally opens the concert." Her eyes were moist with feeling. "Such a brief moment in the sun, before it's all over…"

"Before what's all over?" asked Bruno.

"Why, the concert, of course," said the countess, smoothing an imaginary crease from her skirt. "Whatever else could I have meant?"

She gave a quick demonstration on the piano of Bruno's part. The chords were a little more difficult than anything he had yet attempted, but by the third try he'd just about got it. "One more go," she said and trilled out the melody.

Parp. Parp. Parp. Parpagena, answered Bruno's phartlehorn.

"Fabulous!" cried the countess. "Let's take it from the top!" Bruno bent his legs and prepared to squeeze.

By the end of the piece, both teacher and pupil were breathless with joy. Bruno's heart swelled with emotions he did not quite understand.

"Bravo!" cried the countess, and she shook Bruno's hand in a way that made him feel tremendously grown up. "Your friend Miss Chalk may have been chosen as the solo phartiste, but you're still a fine musician. Now, how about you take your phartlehorn and head back to the dormitory for some practice? I think I need a little time alone with Humbert. After all, there are only two days left until the concert!"

22

The Deepest Phartle of All

Bruno clutched his phartlehorn tight to his chest as he stepped out into the corridor. It was a long walk back to the dormitory, with many narrow, winding stairs to climb, but Bruno didn't care. For the first time since yesterday's disastrous audition there was a spring in his step. Besides, he had a mind to do some exploring on the way.

The castle building was comprised of four hexagonal turrets joined by long rectangular passageways, the walls of which enclosed the internal courtyard. The countess's rooms were located in the south turret and the children's dormitory was in the north. Monsieur Zidler had told them on their first night at the castle that the east turret was strictly off limits to anyone except the duke and his retinue, so that meant Bruno had to travel back via the west turret. It was here that the knights seemed to spend most of their time, and Bruno was keen to know what they got up to when they weren't marching round in circles in the courtyard.

As he approached the heavy tapestry curtain that marked the entrance to the West Tower, Bruno's curiosity began to get the better of him. First checking that no one was coming, he slipped inside. And did a double take. This part of the castle was decorated in a far more modern style than the rest. Stark overhead lighting replaced the candles and chandeliers found elsewhere. Not far from where Bruno was standing was a sealed white doorway. He could hear voices coming from the space beyond, so tiptoeing over, he bent down and put his eye to the keyhole.

To Bruno's disappointment, all he could see on the other side was a rather humdrum-looking office. A handful of knights were sitting behind computers. Others jabbed angrily at photocopiers and printers. There were signed photos of actors and pop stars on the walls. Stacked up in the corner was a vast pile of fireworks. Catherine wheels, roman candles and rockets – all Bruno's favourites were there. He pressed his eye closer to the keyhole. Now, here was something worth investigating. Over in the far corner of the room, a team of knights were gathered around a metal workbench. They were wearing lab coats and goggles, and for some reason they appeared to be slitting open the fireworks and tipping their contents into large plastic buckets. Whatever could they be doing?

Before Bruno had time to observe any more, heavy clogged footsteps sounded down the corridor ahead of him. Quickly, he jumped away from the keyhole and scrambled out through the tapestry curtain.

On his journey back to the North Tower, Bruno paused to inspect several suits of armour, an old spinning globe and a large stuffed tiger. By the time he arrived back at the dormitory, he had quite forgotten about the mystery of the knights and their fireworks.

"Hey," said Grace as Bruno entered, "how was your lesson?"

Shafts of sunlight streaked across the carpet. Grace, Natasha and Xanadu were sitting together on a pile of cushions beside the window. Their faces glowed in the light as they chattered like old friends. Bruno felt a pang of jealousy. Why was Grace so chummy with them all of a sudden?

"Fine, thanks," he said a little coolly and slumped down onto his four-poster bed. "How was yours?"

"It was brilliant!" enthused Grace, coming over to sit next to him. "I know I wasn't sure about phartistry to begin with, but the duke is a really inspiring teacher. Did you know that the phartlehorn is thought to be oldest instrument in the world? Well, anyway, first I learnt the solo from *The Magic Phartlehorn*. Then he taught us all this piece by Tchaikovsky where we got to pretend to be canons. Oh, and I even managed to practise my Phartesian."

"Oh yeah," said Bruno, still sulky. "Let's hear some, then."

"*Tu isicus stillamus mea besticus amigo!*" said Grace, then added quietly, "It means 'you're still my best friend', silly."

"Oh right," said Bruno, blushing. "I knew that."

A day of non-stop music seemed to have put

179

everyone in a good mood. Xanadu leapt up from the floor. "Who wants to hear this track I've been thinking of for my next album?"

The others watched, baffled, as Xanadu knocked his knees together and shuffled his feet apart.

"Why are you standing like you need a pee?" asked Natasha.

Xanadu didn't answer. Instead he reached down for his phartlehorn and swung it up and over his head.

As you've probably realized by now, one of the big differences between a phartlehorn and a normal wind instrument is that it's possible to sing with your mouth while playing one. It was this difference that Xanadu took advantage of now. (Although, between you and me, "sing" might be an over-generous description in this case.)

As he trumped out the tune on his phartlehorn, Xanadu squeaked and ground his way through a love song like a car struggling to change gears.

Bruno put his fingers in his ears. "Stop," he begged. "I can't take any more!"

"Please," squealed Grace, "my tummy's hurting."

"I think I'm going to choke," spluttered Natasha, hiccuping through her nose.

Xanadu pulled off his instrument with a huff. "Well, I'd like to hear you lot try. Bruno couldn't even get a peep of a phartle out at the audition!"

"Oh yeah?" said Bruno, jumping to his feet. "Just listen to this!" He grabbed his own instrument and yanked it down around his body. Then he took a deep breath in before blowing out as hard as he could. The other children were startled into silence. To tell you the truth, even Bruno was a little surprised at the power of the music that now began to erupt spontaneously from his instrument. It was as if the melody emerged from somewhere deep inside. He did not need to think. All he had to do was relax and let the music flow out of him. Closing his eyes, he imagined himself serenading the countess on a starlit beach, the notes from his phartlehorn rising up from the depths of the ocean that lapped at their feet. The other children held their breath as Bruno pressed down on the lowest key.

KABOOM!

The phartle was deeper than the bass on a gangster's car stereo. The walls of the castle shook

in its wake. Bats flapped from the battlements.
Gargoyles crumbled. Water sploshed from the moat
below. From out of the forest came the sound of
a hundred Trumpenhunde, baying in wild delight.

All around the castle, the residents of Phartesia
abandoned their tasks. The cooks in the kitchen,
the grooms in the stable, Monsieur Zidler in the
dungeons, the duke and his moustache-bearers
in the lavatory. All of them stopped to listen as
Bruno's phartle rumbled on and on.

The countess and Humbert both heard it up
in her music room. Immediately deserting her
pupil, Countess Strudel ran towards the source of
the exquisite explosion. When Bruno eventually
opened his eyes, he found himself flat on his face at
her feet, like a sinner bowing before his queen.

The countess was looking down at him in
astonishment. Behind her, Bruno could just about
make out the stunned face of the duke. Strudel
reached down a lily-white hand to help him up.

"The boy's a genius!" she gasped. "Father, he has
to become our new solo phartiste!"

23

An Unofficial Mission

A neon-orange sunset lit up the Mediterranean. The journey from South London by rubbish truck had taken almost twenty-four hours, with Chippy warbling "Ten Green Bottles" all the way. By the time they pulled up outside the Hotel Magnificent, even Grandpa Trevor had begun to lose patience.

Getting Chippy in through the revolving glass door proved to be a tricky business, but eventually the old man managed it. Now he looked around the sparkling lobby in wonder. Mr and Mrs Chalk hovered uncertainly behind him. To think that their daughter had stayed in a palace like this! For a while the three of them just stood there in silence. They had set off full of pluck and courage, but now they'd reached the hotel, no one seemed sure what to do next. The other guests were eyeing Mr Chalk's grubby overalls with suspicion. Mrs Chalk pulled her duffle coat tight about her chest.

Finally Chippy broke the silence. *"Is there any room at the inn?"* she squawked from Grandpa Trevor's shoulder.

He stroked her wing to quiet her. "Shhh! You'll get us thrown out!" But the parrot had sparked an idea in Mrs Chalk.

"The rooms!" she exclaimed. "We should start by having a look at the children's rooms! Didn't Miss Goodwin say they were on the third floor? Maybe there'll be a clue up there."

No one could think of a better plan, so they all bundled into the lift. Just as the doors were about to close, the group was joined by a glamorous young woman in high heels and a bikini. She leant forward and pressed the button marked PENTHOUSE SUITE. Blimey, thought Grandpa Trevor, wondering vaguely if he'd seen her on the television. Mr Chalk's eyes were almost popping out of his head.

"Goodness," he murmured as his wife nudged him out onto the third floor and the lift doors closed behind them. "Wasn't that…?"

"Yes," said Mrs Chalk with a sigh, "it was that young starlet, Desiree Draws. As you can see, she is ninety five per cent recyclable plastic. That was what you were gawping at, wasn't it, dear?"

Mr Chalk nodded meekly as they set off down the corridor. Almost immediately their progress was halted by a barrier of yellow police tape.

"I'm sure this doesn't apply to relatives," said Grandpa Trevor, ducking underneath it and striding on.

The children's rooms had not been touched since the day of their disappearance, and it didn't take long to work out which had been Bruno's. The floor of Room 308 was littered with dirty socks and pants. Damp towels had been left to fester on the bed. Comic books and crisp packets were strewn across the sofa. Tears welled in Grandpa Trevor's eyes. There was no mistaking it, his grandson had been here. Chippy pecked affectionately at the old man's neck.

"I know," said Grandpa Trevor. "You miss him too."

Mrs Chalk appeared in the doorway, red-faced with excitement. "I think I've found something.

Look!" She held out a small white card. "It was in Grace's blazer pocket. The police probably didn't think to look, but I know that's where she always tidies things away."

Grandpa Trevor hurriedly wiped his nose on his sleeve. He took the card from Mrs Chalk.

"*Monsieur Zachary Zidler*," he read uncertainly. "*Impresario.*"

Mrs Chalk was already reaching into her pocket for her mobile phone. Her hands shook as she scrolled through her contacts and pressed dial. It took less than a second for the person on the other end to answer.

"Agent Frogmarch? This is Penelope Chalk. My husband and I are at the Hotel Magnificent with Trevor Pockley... Yes, I know we're not supposed to be in France... Now, there's no need to shout... We think we've found a clue! A business card belonging to a man named Monsieur Zachary Zidler... No, I've never heard of him before... No, no, it's not like Grace to talk to strangers."

An hour later, a large black helicopter touched down on the forecourt of the Hotel Magnificent. Grandpa Trevor's three grey hairs blew up from his head as he ran towards the whirring blades. Mr and Mrs Chalk were right behind him.

Agent Frogmarch hauled herself out through the roof like a genie struggling to escape from a bottle.

"Just give me *one* reason," she bawled, "why I shouldn't have you lot court-marshalled! Meddling in the investigations of Her Majesty's Secret Service is a treasonable offence!"

The two men stared down at the ground like a pair of naughty schoolboys. Perched on Grandpa Trevor's shoulder, Chippy hung her beak in shame. Only Mrs Chalk found the courage to look the special agent in the eye.

"We couldn't just sit at home doing nothing," she protested.

"But that's exactly what I wanted you to do!" shouted Agent Frogmarch. "Luckily for you, your meddling might just have been useful. Otherwise I'd have you all banged up in the tower!"

Mr Chalk didn't like to ask which tower. He scuffed his shoes against the concrete. "Useful?" he said, without raising his head. "In what, erm, way?"

The special agent jumped down from the helicopter and began to pace back and forth in front of them.

"I've run Zidler's name through my intelligence database. It turns out that his passport is registered to a little-known Alpine kingdom called Phartesia. It's been on my suspicious list for a while."

"Phartesia?" repeated Grandpa Trevor. "Well, I'll be blown. In all my days as a sailor, I've never heard of it."

The special agent glared at him. "Phartesia is *landlocked*, you fool. Didn't they teach you geography at school? It's surrounded by land, not sea."

Mrs Chalk put a reassuring hand on Grandpa Trevor's arm. "Well, I've never heard of Phartesia either," she said, "and I backpacked all across Europe before I had Grace."

Agent Frogmarch cracked her knuckles. She was starting to get impatient. "That sounds very intrepid, Mrs Chalk, but you can't *backpack* into Phartesia. Its borders are closed to foreign visitors and heavily guarded with troops."

"Permission to ask, erm, a question," said Mr Chalk.

Agent Frogmarch grunted something which sounded like approval.

"You don't think, do you," said Grace's father,

"that Phartesia might, erm, be the stronghold of the Knights Trumplar?"

The special agent flinched. Her tongue flicked around her lips like a toad preparing to catch a fly. "Have you been hacking into my emails, Mr Chalk?"

"Erm, no," he replied. "It's just that, well, the name Phartesia – it does, erm, sound a bit like those phartlehorns you were telling us about at the meeting..."

His voice was crushed to a whisper under the weight of Agent Frogmarch's stare. "Not just a pretty face, are you, Julian?" she said.

Mr Chalk blushed. "I, erm, well, thanks..."

Agent Frogmarch made a spectacularly strained attempt at a smile. She threw one muscular arm around Grandpa Trevor and the other around both of the Chalks.

"It has occurred to me," she said, drawing them in closer, "that the three of you might be useful to operations after all. My first thought was to parachute into Phartesia myself. But the cretinous head of French secret services has banned it. Apparently one of his agents has already infiltrated the Knights Trumplar and he feels the situation is under control. Bah! As if I'd ever leave the rescue of British citizens to the French! The problem is that if I go in now, it could cause a diplomatic incident…"

She paused, chewing over the possibilities in her mind.

"But I could send you lot in on an unofficial mission instead. Mrs Chalk's idiotic comment about backpacking has given me an idea. You could go in undercover tonight as a party of gormless hitch-hikers who've lost their way. You're just about intelligent enough to pull that off, I think. Your task would be to locate the stronghold of the Knights Trumplar and gather intelligence which could be useful to a British invasion."

Chippy yodelled with excitement.

Agent Frogmarch released her new recruits from her grip. "Obviously the parrot will have to stay at home," she said.

Grandpa Trevor folded his arms across his belly. "Where I go, Chippy goes," he said. "Besides, we'll cover more ground that way. Back in my naval days, I used to send her ahead to scout for land."

Chippy fluttered off into the nearest tree, then quickly returned with a palm frond in her beak.

"Land ahoy! Land ahoy!" she declared, dropping it at Agent Frogmarch's feet.

Now it was Mrs Chalk's turn to object. "I'm sorry to sound negative, Trevor, but don't you think a bright blue parrot might attract a bit of attention in the Alps?"

Grandpa Trevor flashed a tobacco-stained smile. "I've thought of that. I'm not just a pretty face either, you know, Penelope. If we can go in disguise, then why can't Chippy?"

"Twit-twoo," hooted the parrot. "Twit-twoo." Agent Frogmarch's eyes had narrowed to slits. She thrust out a fleshy pink hand and grasped the parrot's claw.

"Welcome to Her Majesty's Secret Service, Agent Chippy. Right then, everybody into the helicopter! There's a secret British intelligence base thirty-two kilometres away from the border with Phartesia. We'll stop off there for your briefing."

24
Dinner with the Duke

Back at the Castle Mistral, Bruno had been honoured with an invitation to dine alone with the duke in the state dining room. Well, not quite alone, for of course the trusty moustache-bearers were there too. They stood behind the duke's throne-like chair, ensuring that the Royal Moustache was kept well clear of his dinner. A crackling fire had been lit in the grate. Shadows danced on the walls, lending movement to the portraits that hung all around the room.

Bruno nervously inspected his cutlery, wondering which of the five silver spoons he was supposed to use. He was a little surprised to note

that while he'd been served his
normal helping of Stunkenstew,
the duke was tucking into a
rosy pink lobster.

"I don't know how you can
stomach that disgusting stuff
myself," he remarked, pointing at Bruno's bowl.

"But I thought Stunkenstew was a Phartesian
delicacy," said Bruno.

One of the trusty moustache-bearers was
coughing loudly. He leant forward and whispered
something into the Royal Ear. The duke flushed.

"Oh!" he burst out. "Is that Stunkenstew you're
eating? Why, of course that's my absolute f-f-
favourite! Alas, doctor's orders mean boring old
lobster for me."

Bruno was more puzzled than ever. Surely
the smell of Stunkenstew was unmistakable?
Especially for someone who'd lived in Phartesia all
their life. The duke hastily changed the subject.

"I only wish," he said, tearing off a lobster claw
and sucking out the flesh, "that my great-great-
great-grandfather Leopold was still alive to hear
you phartle. That's him in the painting over there:
the one with the magnificent nose."

Magnificent was one word for it, thought Bruno. The man's nose was turned up at the end like a drainpipe. The long black nostrils were flared and seemed almost to twitch in the flickering firelight.

"In Leopold's time," the duke continued, "Phartesia was more powerful than either America or China is today. What we lacked in territory, we made up for in influence. People would pay vast sums to attend one of our concerts. Leopold's daughter received no f-f-fewer than f-f-fifteen proposals of marriage, eventually wedding the brother of the King of England. Two hundred years later and look at us! Ever since the prudish ban on phartistry, the world has shunned us. We Knights Trumplar must operate our f-f-fame f-f-factory in secret in order to survive. Do you have any idea how many TV talent shows are run from the west turret of this very castle? How many glittering pop careers we secretly control? Of course not! F-f-for we can only take the money, while others take the glory."

So *that* was what the knights got up to in their office, thought Bruno, suddenly remembering what he'd seen through the keyhole. But what about the fireworks they'd been cutting open? What were they for? Before he had a chance to ask, the conversation had moved on.

"Money is all very well," continued the duke, "but without glory, how am I supposed to f-f-find a suitable husband for Strudel? This, Bruno, is where you come in!"

Bruno's heart leapt. Surely the duke couldn't mean he wanted him to marry Strudel? He was just a boy. But no, of course that was not what the duke meant at all.

"You, Bruno, can help us to reclaim that long-lost glory. When you explode onto the stage, people will have to take notice! Over the years, our secret gala concerts have been gaining in popularity. Each year in May we invite a select handful of celebrities and politicians to Phartesia. These are people who can have anything they want. Pet tigers! Baths of champagne! Holidays in outer space! But soon they grow tired of the shiny baubles of success…"

At first Bruno found this hard to believe – but then he thought of Natasha and how bored she always seemed and he saw the truth in the duke's words.

"Weary of ordinary f-f-forms of entertainment, these celebrities begin to seek out more extreme sources of pleasure. In phartistry, they f-f-find at last what they are searching for! What sweeter music can there be than the sound of a young boy blasting his guts up into the sky?"

Bruno shivered. For the first time since his audition, he felt scared. There was a wild, unhinged look in the duke's eyes. His hands waved about as if he was juggling with invisible knives. For a moment, Bruno considered the possibility that the duke was mad and all his promises of fame and fortune a fantasy. It was too horrible a thought to contemplate, however, so Bruno did what many of us are inclined to do when faced with a terrifying truth. He pushed it straight to the back of his mind. The duke was just passionate, that was all.

Still, Bruno was relieved when the duke stopped talking, picked up a flute from the mantelpiece and blew out the opening three bars of *The Magic Phartlehorn*.

"Strudel tells me she's taught you this already," he said. "Might you be so kind as to duet with me now?"

"Of course!" said Bruno, and reached for his phartlehorn, which was resting on a chair beside him.

196

The duke closed his eyes. With a little bouncing nod of his head, he began to play *The Magic Phartlehorn* again. Bruno waited for the distinctive trill of notes that signalled for him to join in, then, summoning everything he had inside, he blew out into his instrument. A sublime smile spread across the duke's face. For a fleeting second Bruno saw there a resemblance to his beautiful daughter.

As if to challenge Bruno, the duke's playing became faster and faster. Bruno matched him with ease. The phartles popped out of him at machine-gun speed. Parp. Parp. Parp. Parp. Parp. Parp. Parp. Parp. Parp. Parpagena.

The melody danced in the air around them. Then the duke trilled out a final flourish on his flute and the music was over.

"Quite remarkable! I've only one f-f-further piece of advice."

"Yes?" ventured Bruno nervously.

"Do not change a single thing. Play exactly like that at the concert and you will go down in history as the greatest phartiste the world has ever known."

Bruno was speechless. Rarely did he even get a tick in the margin of his homework, let alone a compliment like this! Suddenly he remembered Grandpa Trevor's words when dropping him off for the school trip: "One day you'll be more famous than everyone else at this school put together."

Bruno couldn't wait to tell him he'd been right!

25

Four Go Undercover in Phartesia

Grandpa Trevor counted to ten, then pulled down on the chord of his parachute. He opened his eyes, daring, for the first time, to look down at the ground rushing up to meet his feet. It was difficult to see in the dark, but he could just make out the silhouettes of Mr and Mrs Chalk floating below. He heard a rustle of silk, then felt the weightlessness as his parachute billowed open.

"Wahoooooo!" he cried with a mix of joy and panic as he tried, desperately, to steer himself towards a gap in the trees.

"*Twit-wahoooo!*" echoed Chippy, swooping down alongside him.

The old man
landed with a thud
beside the Chalks. He lay on
the grass, arms thrown back
over his head, panting.

"Blimey!" he gasped.

"I haven't felt that alive since
nineteen sixty-nine! I've got blood rushing to bits
of my body I'd forgotten existed!"

Mr Chalk decided it was time for a hasty change
of subject. "Anyone for a cup of tea?" he asked,
pulling out a thermos.

The three of them were dressed in bobble hats
and Gore-tex jackets. They wore stout walking
boots and knee-high socks held up with garters.
Thanks to Scotland Yard's experts in avian disguise,
Chippy had been transformed from a blue-and-
yellow parrot into a tawny owl. While the others
struggled to put up the tent in the dark, Chippy
flew off into the forest to practise her hoot.

"There we go," said Mr Chalk, banging in the final peg. "That should do it! I think it looks rather cosy."

Awoooooooo, awoooooooooo.

Mr Chalk dropped his mallet on his toe. He hopped around the tent, groaning and cursing. "Blasted boxer shorts!" he shouted. "What was that?"

Awooooooooo, awooooooooooo.

There it was again: a wild baying sound coming from deep in the forest.

"Chippy?" called Grandpa Trevor. "Is that you?"

Awoooooooo, awooooooooooo, awoooooooo, awooooooooooo.

"Stop it at once, you naughty bird!" the old man warned. "You're supposed to be an owl, not a werewolf!"

Hooting with indignation, Chippy floated down from her perch on a nearby pine tree. "Twit-twoo," she hooted. "Twit-twoo!"

Mrs Chalk frowned. "I don't think it was Chippy. That noise was further off. Hang on a minute, this might help."

She reached into her backpack for Agent Frogmarch's briefing notes, then scanned down the pages with her torch. Since no one from British intelligence had managed to penetrate Phartesia in a hundred years, the notes were based on historical accounts of the kingdom and were quite old-fashioned – but, still, they were better than nothing.

"Aha! Here's what we need: *Wild Animals of Phartesia*."

"What does it say?" asked Grandpa Trevor, peering down into the puddle of yellow light. "See anything that fits the bill?"

"Well it wasn't a marmoset," said Mrs Chalk, "or a roe deer or a fox or a rabbit. And it definitely wasn't a hedgehog! So, according to this, it can only have been … a *Trumpenhund*!"

"A Trumpenhund?" repeated her husband. "What the blinking heck is that?"

Mrs Chalk read aloud from the notes:

"*Originating from the remote mountains of Phartesia, the Trumpenhund is the world's rarest breed of dog. Instantly recognizable by its enormous nostrils and shaggy white beard, the Trumpenhund is prized by the Knights Trumplar for its exceptional olfactory abilities.*"

"Exceptional olfactory abilities." Grandpa Trevor scratched his head through his hat. "You've lost me. What does that mean?"

202

"It means it has a really good sense of smell," explained Mr Chalk. "I wonder what they use it for? Hunting rabbits, perhaps?"

Mrs Chalk read on in a grim voice.

"Whilst famous for its loyalty to its master, the wild Trumpenhund is a truly dangerous beast. At the turn of the last century, it was estimated that three hundred of the creatures roamed free in the forests of Phartesia. Nobody knows how many of these terrible creatures might still be living there today. Uncorroborated reports suggest that their jaws are strong enough to savage a bear with a single—" She flipped off her torch. "Best I don't read any more."

"Curse that helmet-haired woman!" Mr Chalk burst out. "I bet that story about the French banning her from coming here was just an excuse. If you ask me, she's plain scared!"

Awooooooo, awoooooooooo, came the sound from the forest.

26

The Hexagonal Chamber

Bruno lay wide awake in bed replaying the day's events over and over in his mind, like a film in which he was the star. Thinking too hard about the duke's strange behaviour at dinner made him feel uneasy. Instead he focused on his lesson with the countess and his surprise promotion to solo phartiste. To his relief, Grace had confided that since she'd never wanted to be famous anyway, she didn't mind giving up the role.

From across the room there came a rustle of covers, followed by the *pad, pad, pad* of bare feet on wooden floorboards. Bruno rolled over just in time to see Humbert slipping out through the door.

Where was he going? The bathroom was in the other direction, so that couldn't be it. Bruno threw back his covers and scurried across to Grace's bed.

"Wake up," he whispered, gently shaking her shoulders.

Grace rubbed her eyes. "What is it?" she groaned.

"Shhhh…" Bruno raised his finger to his lips. "Humbert's sneaked off somewhere. I'm going to follow him. Find out what's he up to. You coming?"

Grace shoved back her covers, fully awake now. "You bet!"

Careful not to wake the others, Bruno and Grace crept out into the corridor. At night, the castle was a cold and forbidding place. Moonlight streamed in through the archers' windows, casting long shadows on the ground. The only sound to be heard was the distant baying of Trumpenhunde in the forest below. Humbert was nowhere to be seen.

"Which way do you think he went?" asked Grace, baffled.

They were standing on a small stone landing. Directly in front of them was the staircase that led down into the dining hall. Off to their right was the corridor that led to the west turret and the offices of the Knights Trumplar. To their left was the corridor that led to the duke's quarters in the East Tower.

"Er, that way?" suggested Bruno, pointing left.

"That's my hunch too," said Grace.

So off they set towards the East Tower. They had barely gone two metres, however, when Bruno jumped backwards in fright. A huge figure loomed out of the moonlit gloom, wielding an axe.

"It's only a suit of armour, you numpty," said Grace. "Perhaps I'd better go first."

It wasn't long before they reached the end of the corridor. A heavy tapestry curtain, similar to that which Bruno had crept through earlier in the day, hung across the entrance to the East Tower. Grace pulled back a corner of the fabric then slipped through. Bruno followed. The curtain closed behind them with a swoosh.

No moonlight shone into the windowless space beyond. It took a moment for the children's eyes to adjust. Then they froze.

Slouched in a chair opposite was a high-ranking knight. His moustache trailed down to the floor, where Bruno could just about make out the silhouette of a quietly slumbering

Trumpenhund. The knight's head was tipped back at an uncomfortable angle. For a second, Bruno wondered if he was dead, but then his head jerked forward and he let out a mighty rumbling snore.

"He's fast asleep," Grace said softly. "Let's get going before he wakes up!"

Bruno expected her to head back through the curtain, but instead she struck out towards the sleeping knight.

"W-w-what are you doing?" he whispered.

"I can see a staircase." She pointed into the gloom. "Over there, behind his chair."

Reluctantly, Bruno followed as Grace hopped over the knight's trailing moustache, tiptoed past the slumbering Trumpenhund and began to descend the stairs.

If it had been dark at the top, halfway down the spiral staircase it was darker still. Bruno held on tight to the banister as the steps grew cold beneath his bare feet. It felt as if they were descending to the centre of the earth.

"*Ouch!*" said Grace, stopping suddenly.

In the darkness she had stumbled face first into a wooden door. A flicker of light glowed around the door frame. Determined to prove that he could be brave, Bruno tried the handle.

To his surprise the door creaked open, revealing a large hexagonal chamber. The room was empty, but someone must have visited recently, for freshly lit candles burned in candelabras on the wall. In the centre of the room was a round stone table encircled by thirteen golden chairs.

Tentatively Bruno stepped in over the threshold, with Grace following close behind. Bruno took a candle from its holder, and together they began to look around. The walls were lined with rows and rows of black-and-white photographs. Curious, Bruno lifted the candle to the nearest picture. Five children with buck teeth and pudding-bowl haircuts grinned out at him. They were posing outside the castle with their phartlehorns. A neatly printed inscription read: SUMMER 1978.

"These must be photos from previous concerts," said Bruno, turning to Grace. "There are hundreds of them."

"One for every year?" she suggested.

For a while they wandered idly about the chamber inspecting more of the photographs.

"What do you reckon happened to them?" mused Grace. "You'd think that if there were this many trained phartistes in the world, it would be hard to keep secret."

"Who knows," said Bruno. "Maybe they just hang out with each other being rich and famous. Look, this one's different. Here they're not just posing, they're playing."

Grace peered over his shoulder. "They look even more swollen than we do after a bowl of Stunkenstew," she observed.

Bruno held up the candle to the next photograph. He let out a gasp of shock. "They're not just swollen! They're going up in puffs of smoke!"

Grace snatched the candle from his hand. "What? Let me see!"

Bruno was right. Phartlehorns were hurtling through the air. Where there should have been children, there was nothing but wispy clouds of smoke. In the Royal Box, a younger duke was clapping wildly. A very young Monsieur Zidler, unmistakable with his oiled black hair and a Trumpenhund at his side, had his arms thrown back, his face bathed in ecstasy. The Countess Strudel, aged about five or six, was doing a jig of joy.

Bruno and Grace retreated slowly from the photographs.

"M-m-maybe it was an accident?" stammered Bruno.

"Uh-uh." Grace shook her head. "You saw the audience. They weren't panicking. They were *celebrating!*"

She swept the candle around the room. Bruno took another sharp intake of breath. There were dozens of photos all showing the same thing. Children evaporating into puffs of smoke! The audience ecstatic!

Suddenly the duke's words began to ring in Bruno's ears. *Blown away by the boy's talent… Explosive performance… Your name blasted into the stars…*

To Bruno's dismay, he realized that the clues had been there all along. He'd simply been too dazzled by compliments to hear them. Most painful of all came the memory of the countess sitting at her piano. *Such a brief moment in the sun, before it's all over,* she had said. Bruno wanted to kick himself. How could he have been so foolish?

"Grace!" he exclaimed. "We're not here to become rich and famous, are we? We're here to be…"

He couldn't bring himself to finish the sentence.

A moment or two passed and the two children remained rooted to the spot. Then Bruno grabbed Grace by the hand and pulled her towards the door.

"If the knights catch us here, who knows what they'll do! We need to get back to the dormitory and warn the others."

As fast as they could, the pair ran back up the staircase, their feet pelting against the stone. Halfway up they heard the sound of distant chanting. Grace grabbed at the sleeve of Bruno's pyjamas.

"Stop!" she whispered. "Listen!"

The chanting grew louder and heavy clogged footsteps could now be heard thundering down the steps above them. Bruno looked at Grace: the staircase offered no other way out. All they could do was return to the chamber and search for

somewhere to hide there. Hand in hand, they raced
back down the stairs and looked around the room
in a panic.

"Quick!" hissed Bruno. "The table!"

They hurled themselves under ... just in time.
Then the door opened.

27

The Explosive Elixir

The Grand Council of the Knights Trumplar filed into the hexagonal chamber. From their hiding place the children could see only the knights' legs, in their turquoise silk tights and pompommed clogs. Once again, they were chanting in unison:

> "Et volcanicus erupticus exquisiticus,
> In revengicus pharticus apocalypsum
> Plus ferocicus que un turnipum
> Childrenicus explodicus annulis."

Grace dropped her head into her hands. "I'm so sorry," she whispered to Bruno. "I should have worked out earlier what they were singing. I pretended to understand because I wanted you to think I was better at Phartesian than I really am."

Bruno was astonished. Fancy Grace wanting to impress him! But this was not the time to quiz her about it. "You understand now, right?"

Grace nodded meekly. "Basically, it means we're history…"

Bruno squeezed her hand as the Grand Council of the Knights Trumplar took their seats at the table. It was clear that these were very senior knights: their moustaches trailed across the floor like the silvery fronds of a spider's web. A web on which the children were trapped like flies. All it would take would be for one fidgety knight to stretch out his legs, or for someone to drop something under the table, and they'd be discovered.

Someone began shouting in Phartesian. Bruno recognized the pompous voice of the duke. Thankfully, during recent days Grace's grasp of the language had indeed improved dramatically. She was able to provide Bruno with a pretty accurate translation, which for the sake of time I shall paraphrase for you here.

"The day after tomorrow," the duke began, "our famous friends will flock to this glorious kingdom. This is Phartesia's chance to prove that we are still a force to be reckoned with. I am relying on you, my trusted advisors, to ensure the party goes with a bang!"

The knights roared with laughter. Grace winced as she relayed the duke's words to Bruno.

"Don't worry," he assured her. "We'll be long gone by then."

"As always," continued the duke, "the evening will begin with canapés in the courtyard. The concert will commence with an aria from *The Magic Phartlehorn*. Then we'll have an extract from 'Air on the G String', followed by the first movement of Wagner's Ring Cycle. The finale will be a performance of Tchaikovsky's 1812 Overture. The children will phartle the parts of the canons. *Boom! Boom! Boom!* We will blast them into the sky!"

The knights stomped their clogs in approval. Grace gave a quick translation. Bruno shivered to think how desperate he'd been to impress the duke only yesterday. How he'd lapped up the countess's compliments. When all the while they'd been planning on sending him up in smoke!

The duke's tone had turned serious.

"He's introducing Sir Oswald, his Chief of Security," explained Grace.

The knight nearest to Bruno rose to his feet.

215

The pompoms on his shoes were a bright daffodil yellow. He spoke extremely slowly, with long, ponderous pauses.

"By carelessly kidnapping such high-profile children … Monsieur Zidler has put us all in most grave danger… Kidnap the son of a peasant and no one notices … kidnap a rich man's son and the whole world takes an interest. As you know, a huge reward has been offered for the children…" Sir Oswald chuckled to himself. "Thankfully our famous friends are *far* too rich to be tempted by this… More worrying are the rumours circulating on the Internet of a possible rescue attempt."

The knights murmured in dismay. Bruno looked quizzically at Grace.

"Good news," she said. "We're going to be rescued!"

"Therefore," continued Sir Oswald, "I've trebled security patrols in the forest. No one gets in or out of Phartesia without my knowing." The Chief of Security sat back down at the table. The colour had drained from Grace's face.

"What's wrong?" asked Bruno.

"Scratch that. No rescue mission. We're on our own."

Now the duke spoke again. It sounded as if he was barking out a set of orders. Sir Oswald stood up to reply.

"What are they saying?" hissed Bruno, frustrated.

"They're talking about an 'explosive elixir'," replied Grace, straining to listen. "It's a potion… Something they've been making from fireworks… They're going to give it to us before the concert… They're planning to poison us!"

Bruno remembered the knights he'd seen hard at work in the West Tower and felt sick. They'd been cutting up fireworks! Why hadn't he thought to mention it to anyone?

The duke bellowed a final command. "Bring out the prisoner!" translated Grace.

The hidden pair heard a rattle of chains, followed by the **clank, clank, clank** of a person walking in shackles. Then the prisoner, whoever he was, began to scream. It sounded to Bruno as if he was begging for mercy.

"It's Monsieur Zidler!" gasped Grace. "The duke says he had been planning on testing the explosive potion on some other prisoners he's got rotting in the dungeon. But he's changed his mind and now

217

he's going to test it on Zidler..."

Bruno and Grace heard the sound of a struggle followed by a terrified snivelling. The Grand Council of the Knights Trumplar swivelled round in their seats, waiting with bated breath. Too curious to resist, Bruno quietly crawled forward and peeked out from between the circle of legs.

There was Monsieur Zidler, cowering in the corner. Sir Oswald was just replacing a small glass bottle into a cupboard behind the duke's throne. Already, the talent scout's belly had swollen to ten times its normal size. He looked like a skittle waiting to be struck down by a tenpin bowl.

The seconds ticked by.

Monsieur Zidler's face flushed from pink to purple to puce. Then, one by one, the silver buttons popped from his waistcoat and pinged around the chamber. The last button skidded across the floor, spun on its edge and came to a halt right by Bruno's hand.

"Un souveniricus!" laughed Sir Oswald and bent down to retrieve the button. Bruno felt a surge of panic as the knight's fingers almost grazed his arm. Just in time, he retreated back into the shadows.

The duke was now counting down from ten:

"Tenicus, ninicus, eighticus, sevenicus, sixicus, fivicus, fouricus, threeicus, twoicus, ONEICUS!"

Suddenly it was as if the room had been hit by a subterranean earthquake. The children clutched onto the table leg, praying they would not be crushed beneath its heavy stone top.

Then, silence.

The floor of the chamber was covered in an ash-white dust. Grace's eyes watered as she fought back a sneeze. The knights leapt to their feet, whooping and hollering. Grace gave in to her allergy. *Atchoo, Atchoo, Atchoo,* she sneezed. But the noise was drowned out by the rejoicing of the Knights Trumplar.

Bruno waited for a moment or two longer, then crawled forward again. Monsieur Zidler was nowhere to be seen. Where he had stood, there was nothing but a thick pile of ash and a whiff of burnt toast and hair oil.

The duke was cackling with delight. "Jobsworth!" he shouted.

As if by magic, the butler's clogs appeared in the entrance to the chamber. He was carrying a broom.

The duke strode over to the doorway, still issuing orders in Phartesian. The trusty moustache-bearers scuttled after him. The knights resumed their chanting as they marched up the stairs behind the duke.

"Et volcanicus erupticus exquisiticus,
In revengicus pharticus apocalypsum..."

Jobsworth hummed along as he swept up what remained of Monsieur Zidler. The broom stirred up the dust beneath the table. Grace, determined not to let out another sneeze, clamped her fingers tightly over her nose until, finally, Jobsworth snuffed out the candles and was gone.

The children counted to a hundred, then crept out into the darkness. It was time to tell the others the terrible news.

Hatching the Plan

Natasha, Xanadu, Bruno and Grace huddled together inside the curtains of Bruno's four-poster bed. Behind them, Humbert's bed was still empty.

As calmly as he could, Bruno explained how he'd seen Humbert sneak out from the dormitory. He told how he and Grace had decided to follow him; how they'd crept past the sleeping knight to enter the forbidden east turret. Next he described the spiral staircase that led down to the hexagonal chamber. Then, finally, Bruno told the others about the photographs of children going up in smoke, and how he and Grace had watched as the knights tested the explosive elixir on Monsieur Zidler.

"Holy moley!" said Xanadu. For the first time in nine years, he removed his sunglasses. Beneath them his eyes were a piercing electric green. He stared directly at Bruno. "We've got to do a runner."

Grace hugged her pyjama-clad knees to her chest. She shook her head. "The knights are patrolling the forest. No one gets in or out of Phartesia without them knowing, that's what Sir Oswald said."

Natasha hammered her fist into the mattress. Her plait swung behind her like a whip. "Have you got a better idea?"

"Actually," said Grace, "I think I have."

Bruno stared at her in surprise.

"Listen," said Grace, "my mum says Plan A is to run away from trouble as fast as you can. But we can't run away because we're surrounded. So it's time for Plan B."

"Which is?" demanded Natasha.

"That attack is the best means of defence!" replied Grace. "The Knights Trumplar want to blow us up. I say we turn the tables and blow *them* up instead!"

"Genius!" exclaimed Xanadu, then looked crestfallen. "But how?"

"The explosive elixir!" said Bruno, suddenly guessing. "They're planning to sprinkle it into our dinner. If we steal it, we can pour it into *their* food!"

Grace beamed at him and raised her hand for a high five.

"Sorry to break up the party," cut in Natasha, "but won't the knights notice that the potion's gone?"

"That's easy," said Bruno with a smile. "We replace it with a fake."

"But how will we get the potion into the knights' food?" asked Xanadu. "They never eat with us."

Bruno frowned. "Good point," he admitted.

There was a squeak of floorboards out in the corridor.

"Someone's coming," hissed Natasha. "Quick! Back to bed!"

The children raced across the dormitory. Bruno hurriedly rearranged his covers, trying his best to look asleep.

A figure appeared in the doorway. The children held their breath.

"You don't fool me," sneered a familiar voice. "But why are you lot up? Shouldn't you be letting your precious instruments get some rest?"

Bruno's heart rate began to slow again. Humbert! "What are *we* doing up?" he said indignantly. "More like what are *you* doing up? You've been gone for hours! Grace and I tried to follow you. And it's a good job we did, too! It turns out we're in massive danger."

Humbert looked confused. "Danger?"

Natasha sat up in bed, as straight-backed as a vampire rising from her coffin. "We're not here for a concert," she snapped. "We've been kidnapped."

To everyone's surprise, a rare genuine smile lit up Humbert's face. "But that's really cool!" he exclaimed. "We'll be all over the papers! They'll probably even make a film about us."

"Aren't you worried?" asked Grace, propping herself up on her elbows.

Humbert shrugged. "Why should I be worried? If we've been kidnapped, my parents will simply pay a ransom. Then I'll be set free. I wonder if they'll let me play myself in the movie."

Bruno decided to cut to the chase. "They don't want a ransom," he said. "They want to blow us up."

"Blow us *up*?" scoffed Humbert, "Don't be ridiculous. It's mad enough that these lunatics

224

want us to blow *off*. They'd never dare to blow us *up*!"

Xanadu slipped out from where he'd been hiding behind a curtain.

"Where are your sunglasses?" asked Humbert, shocked.

"Dude, this is no time to talk fashion. The knights have a special potion. Bruno and Grace saw them test it on Monsieur Zidler. He exploded right in front of them! We've been trying to think of a way to put the potion into the knights' food before it gets into ours."

Humbert clambered back into his bed. He plumped up his pillows. "Well, why didn't you just say that in the first place? That's easy. All you have to do is sprinkle it over their canapés."

"What are canapés?" asked Bruno.

"Those little nibbly things people eat at parties," said Humbert. "But you wouldn't know about sophisticated stuff like that, would you, Stink Bomb?"

Bruno's fists clenched into tight balls of anger. Grace shot him a restraining look as Humbert waved a dismissive hand in the air.

"I still think you're overreacting. But, if you

must know, I think the palace cooks have already made the canapés for the concert. I've just been in the kitchens and seen them all stacked up in the fridges."

A very small part of Bruno wanted to throw his arms around Humbert.

"What were you doing in the kitchens?" asked Natasha.

Humbert looked a little embarrassed. "None of your business," he sniped. (Between you and me, what Humbert wasn't going to admit was that he'd been down in the kitchens trying to steal some Stunkenstew, in the hope that an extra portion might improve his phartling.)

Grace leant forward like a small, earnest general briefing her troops. "OK, so here's what we do," she said. "We go down to breakfast and get through the dress rehearsal as if nothing's wrong. We wait until tomorrow night, when everyone's asleep, to make our move. Xanadu, Natasha and I will stay here and create a diversion. Humbert, you'll go with Bruno…"

"Why do I have to go with *him*?" the two boys protested together.

Grace folded her arms across her chest. "It has

to be you two," she said. "Bruno knows the way to the chamber, Humbert knows where to find the canapés. First stop the chamber, to steal the elixir. Then you'll head to the kitchens to pour it over the canapés. I'd go myself, but it's too risky. I almost gave us away *twice* tonight by sneezing, remember?"

The two boys glared at each other.

"I still don't believe a word of this," said Humbert. "But anything to relieve the boredom of being holed up in here for another day."

29

The Trap

Grandpa Trevor unzipped the flap of his tent and crawled out into the dew-soaked morning. Chippy fluttered out behind him. The grass was studded with buttercups and daisies. There was birdsong in the trees and the sky was a perfect forget-me-not blue. How strange, thought Trevor Pockley, that the sun should continue to shine so brightly when he felt as if his whole world had fallen apart.

A little way off, Mr and Mrs Chalk were already busy frying up some freeze-dried sausages on a portable stove.

"Right then," said Mrs Chalk after they'd breakfasted and packed away the tents. "I guess we'd better get the map out and decide where we're heading."

Grandpa Trevor peered at the map over her shoulder. It showed no paths or villages, only a vast, uninterrupted stretch of forest. He scratched his bald head in confusion.

"If this is the *kingdom* of Phartesia, surely somewhere there should be a castle."

"Good point," agreed Mr Chalk, "but where?"

Chippy hooted from a branch above. She flapped her brown-and-white wing extensions.

"I'm the king of the castle!" she squawked. "I'm the king of the castle! Get down, you dirty rascal! Get down, you dirty rascal!"

"Cut it out, Chippy," scolded Grandpa Trevor. "You're supposed to be an owl, remember. Owls can't talk."

"Hang on a minute," said Mr Chalk. "I think Chippy's trying to tell us something." He jumped up onto a tree stump and shouted at the top of his voice:

"I'm the king of the castle, get down you dirty rascal!"

Mrs Chalk nervously approached her husband. She spoke in a soothing voice. "Julian, darling, I think you may be suffering from hysteria. We're all deeply worried, but playing children's games won't help."

"Don't be daft, Penny." Mr Chalk jumped down from the tree stump. "I'm not hysterical. In fact, my head's never felt clearer. Don't you see? In the game, the castle must always be higher than the rascal. It's the same in real life. Rulers always build their castles at the highest point in the kingdom. That way they get to look down on everyone else!"

"Which means," said Mrs Chalk, hurriedly consulting the map, "that the castle of Phartesia ..."

"...must be up there!" cried Grandpa Trevor, pointing up at the highest peak. "Julian, you're a genius!"

Chippy hooted in protest.

"I already knew *you* were a genius, Chippy," he added, giving the bird a thumbs-up.

Mr Chalk fished around in his pockets for his binoculars. He focused them on the summit of the mountain. "Blinking heck!" he cried. "I can see it! Look, there, half-hidden behind those trees.

It's built right into the mountainside." He passed the binoculars to Grandpa Trevor.

"Well, I'll be darned." The old man whistled. "Just look at all those turrets! That's a mighty long way up to build a castle."

"There must be a road that leads up there," said Mrs Chalk, still poring over the map.

Mr Chalk was already packing up his rucksack. "No time to hunt around for roads," he said. "Even if there is one, it's sure to wind its way all around the mountain. It'll be much quicker just to climb straight up."

Grandpa Trevor exhaled deeply. In places the cliff face looked almost vertical. To be honest, he wasn't sure his creaky joints were up to it.

"Where there's a will, there's a way," chirped Chippy.

"That's the spirit!" said Mrs Chalk, stuffing the map back into her pocket.

The trek started out easily enough. The ground was firm underfoot and the incline was not too steep. Mr Chalk snapped off a willow branch and used it to cut a swathe through the undergrowth. Now and again he would startle a partridge and send it whirring away into the sky. Once, Chippy hooted in fright as an eagle dropped like a stone in front of them, swooping back up with a rabbit clutched between its claws. Other than that, in two hours of walking they saw no living creatures at all.

While the Chalks were desperate to set eyes on their daughter, they knew that the old man was struggling to keep up. They stuck to a steady pace and paused often for water.

"Plenty more where that came from," said Mrs Chalk, offering Grandpa Trevor the last swig from her bottle. "Next stream we come to, we'll refill."

It wasn't long before they heard the gurgle of water. It came from a clearing beyond the trees.

"Stick close together," said Mr Chalk beating back a patch of bracken and nettles, "that way you won't get stu— Aarghhhhh!"

All at once, the three of them felt the ground collapse beneath their feet. They went tumbling down through thin air, landing in a heap at the bottom of a deep pit. Chippy hooted in alarm, then fluttered down to join them. Grandpa Trevor tried to stand up but his ankle gave way beneath him.

Mr and Mrs Chalk rose unsteadily to their feet and looked up. The sides of the pit were at least four metres high.

"Looks like we're in big trouble," moaned Mr Chalk, inspecting the pile of bracken that had fallen in on top of them. "This trap was freshly laid. Whoever dug it will be back before long. And from what Agent Frogmarch told us about the people who live here…" He drew his finger across his throat.

Tears welled in Mrs Chalk's eyes. "I don't care what happens to us," she sniffed. "But what about Grace and Bruno? Who's going to rescue them now?"

Grandpa Trevor was thinking fast. There was no mobile phone reception in Phartesia – Agent Frogmarch had forgotten about that problem. But perhaps there was another way to get a message out. "Penelope, have you got a pen and paper?"

"Here you go," she said, wiping away her tears and pulling out a notepad and pen from her rucksack.

Grandpa Trevor tore off a long thin strip of paper. First he drew a picture of the castle nestling into the mountaintop. (Funnily enough, it displayed a surprising amount of artistic skill.) Next to the castle he wrote: HEAD HERE FIRST TO RESCUE THE CHILDREN!

Then, as an afterthought, he added a drawing of the pit and the words: We are trapped here, please come and rescue us next if you have the time!

When his drawing was complete, Grandpa Trevor turned to Mrs Chalk and said, "Give me your hairband."

Mrs Chalk stared at his bald scalp in confusion.

"It's not for me," he added impatiently.

Penelope Chalk pulled the band from her ponytail and handed it to Grandpa Trevor, who summoned Chippy to his knee. Carefully, the old man wrapped the paper around the parrot's claw, then fixed it in place with the elastic. He spoke to the bird in a gentle voice.

"It's up to you now, Chippy. I need you to fly back down to base. Get this message to Agent Frogmarch."

The parrot cocked her head. Clearly she didn't want to leave the old man's side.

"Please, Chippy," urged Grandpa Trevor. "You're our only hope."

Chippy fluttered her wings and let out a warbling screech. "Ain't no mountain high enough! Ain't no valley low enough," she sang, fluttering up into the air, "to keep me from you-oooo!"

With a last look back at Grandpa Trevor, Chippy sailed away into the sky. Mr and Mrs Chalk watched in amazement.

"Do you think she'll make it?" asked Mrs Chalk.

"Of course she will," said Grandpa Trevor proudly. "Agent Frogmarch will be up at that castle in no time. Whether she makes it back here in time to rescue us is another question."

The Waiting

The first part of Grace's plan shouldn't have been too difficult to pull off, for it simply involved acting normal. Yet acting normal proved easier said than done. At breakfast the next morning the children struggled to keep the fear from their faces.

Acting naturally during the dress rehearsal in the Phartling Hall proved even tougher. Even if they hadn't known about the knights' terrible plot, it would still have been a strange occasion. The children stood together on a little raised platform in the centre of the stage. A grand piano had been wheeled out, and the Countess Strudel now sat at it, fingers poised over the keys. The duke conducted from the Royal Box. A few paces behind him stood the trusty moustache-bearers, pulling back his whiskers like a pair of reins.

"When I point at you," the duke instructed the children, "it's time to phartle out your part. Right, let's start with *The Magic Phartlehorn*. Bruno, after last night's performance I'm expecting nothing short of perfection."

Yesterday, nothing would have made Bruno happier than taking centre stage. Today it took all his acting skills to muster a smile. All his life Bruno had loved parping. Finally he'd thought his talents might be appreciated. He'd dared to dream he could live the life of a famous phartiste. But it had all turned out to be a lie. The Knights Trumplar weren't just passionate about parping – they were mad about murder.

Now, Bruno stared out at the magnificent hall and longed to be safe at home aboard *The Jolly Codger* with Chippy and his Grandpa Trevor. More than anything he yearned to be reunited with his parents. But that, he thought sadly, would happen only in heaven. Somehow his sadness found an outlet in his phartling.

Parp, parp, parp, parpagena, sang his

phartlehorn, and the notes were mournful, rich and low.

"Bravo!" cried the duke when the piece came to an end. "I'd never have thought it possible, but that was even better than yesterday. Phartle like that tomorrow and you'll blow the audience away!"

Bruno wanted to scream with anger, "Your little jokes don't fool me! I know what you're planning!" But what good would it do? They were outnumbered twenty to one. Grace was right. Their only chance was to try to act normal. With a heavy heart he listened to the countess strike up the next tune.

The duke made the children play each piece over and over until he was satisfied that it was perfect, and the dress rehearsal dragged on until dinner. After another quick bowl of Stunkenstew the children were sent straight to their dormitory. Now there was nothing to do but wait until it got dark. The hours dragged on and on. The atmosphere grew tenser and tenser. Bruno and Grace tried to while away the hours by playing cards. Xanadu helped Natasha to braid her hair. Humbert picked his nose.

"What if the boys get caught?" fretted Natasha.

"What if they can't find the potion?" worried Xanadu.

"Guys!" said Grace, exasperated. "Will you please try to think positive!"

Bruno said nothing. He was determined not to show it, but inside he was more nervous than any of them.

At last the sun began to sink below the horizon. In a few hours, the knights would go to bed and it would be time to put the second part of Grace's plan into action.

Eight hours had passed since Grandpa Trevor and the Chalks had fallen into the pit. As darkness fell over the mountain, noises could be heard in the clearing above. First there was a soft snuffling sound, followed by an eerie bleating. Then a long, elegant head peered down into the hole. Everybody in the pit breathed out in relief. A deer. The animal blinked at them for a few seconds before wandering away into the forest.

"Beautiful creature," said Mr Chalk with a sigh. "She probably came to drink from the stream."

"This is hopeless," complained Mrs Chalk. "We can't just sit here waiting for Agent Frogmarch.

What if she hasn't made it to the castle yet? Anything could be happening to the children."

An idea was beginning to form in Grandpa Trevor's mind. He wasn't sure it would work, but it had to be worth a shot. With a huge creaking effort, he crouched down until his head was level with Mr Chalk's bottom.

"Hop onto my shoulders, Julian," he invited.

"A piggyback?" asked Mr Chalk, incredulous.

"Not just a piggyback," declared Grandpa Trevor. "A human pyramid!"

Mr and Mrs Chalk looked at the old man as if he was mad, but he wasn't to be put off.

"OK – so it's not *technically* a pyramid. More like a human ladder. Penny, when Julian's on my shoulders you'll have to find a way to climb up onto his. Then you can scramble out of this hole and find a rope or something to haul us boys out. We'll storm the castle tonight!"

"Or how about I just escort you there myself?" came a gravelly voice above their heads.

Grandpa Trevor and the Chalks froze. Slowly, they raised their eyes to the top of the pit. To their dismay, they found themselves surrounded by a circle of brightly coloured pompomed clogs.

31

Making the Swap

The second part of Grace's plan was what is commonly known as a diversion. All that day, the children had been gathering small objects from around the castle: teaspoons, pepperpots, bars of soap – whatever they could get their hands on. These objects were now piled up on a table in the dormitory. They had blown out all the candles so that no one would suspect they were still awake, and it was almost as dark inside the dormitory as it was outside.

Natasha, Xanadu and Humbert were whispering together in a corner, awaiting instructions. Bruno watched as Grace grabbed a spoon and threw it as hard as she could out of the window. It landed with a **splosh!** in the moat below.

"We'll keep lobbing these out until you're back," she said, peering out into the darkness. "That should keep the knights distracted."

Far below, two armed knights were already running over to investigate.

"Unidentified flying object in the moat!" they called in Phartesian. "Possible intruder alert! Possible intruder alert!"

Grace tapped Bruno on the shoulder. "Here," she said, "you'll need these." She shoved two plastic water bottles into his hands. One was empty, the other was full. Bruno looked at them blankly.

"What do I do with these?" he asked. Grace tapped her pixie nose with a smile. Bruno got the impression she was beginning to enjoy her new-found leadership skills.

"Think about it…" she said.

Suddenly the penny dropped. Bruno's grin stretched from ear to ear. "I get it! I pour the elixir into the empty bottle. Then I replace it with the water from the full one. Grace, you're a genius!"

Grace tucked a wayward strand of hair behind her ear. "Thanks," she said, blushing. "Now, quick, it's time for you and Humbert to get going."

At the sound of his name, Humbert strolled

over. "Come on then, Stink Bomb," he sneered. "Let's go and see this Chamber of Horrors. Exploding children! What a load of tosh! I'll believe it when I see it."

"You bet you will," said Bruno.

Armed with only a candle and the two plastic water bottles, the boys set off down the corridor. Having come this way once already, Bruno was less jumpy than he'd been last night. Soon they were at the entrance to the East Tower.

"With any luck," said Bruno, "the knight will be asleep. If not, you'll have to think of something to distract him while I make a run for it."

Gingerly, Bruno pulled back the curtain. From the far side of the room there came a loud drilling sound.

"Yikes," said Humbert, sticking his fingers in his ears. "What's that?"

"That," replied Bruno, "is a good sign. He's snoring. The staircase is right behind his chair. All we have to do is creep past. I'll go first."

Keeping his back pressed against the wall, Bruno skirted round the edge of the chamber. Reaching the top of the staircase, he turned to

243

check on Humbert. Bruno couldn't believe it. He was sauntering across the middle of the room, as relaxed as if he was taking a stroll around the St Ermingarda's school playground! Didn't he realize the knight could wake up at any moment?

And then, to Bruno's dismay, he did.

Abruptly, the snoring stopped. The knight sat bolt upright in his chair. His eyes flipped open. For a second he seemed to stare directly at Humbert. Then his chin fell back to his chest. The snoring started again, louder than ever. Humbert scampered towards the stairs.

"That was close!" He laughed.

"Close?" gasped Bruno. "You almost had us killed! Now, come on."

"So this is the way to the Chamber of Horrors," scoffed Humbert as they descended down into the gloom. "I bet you and Grace imagined it all. Scared of the dark, that'd be my guess."

Bruno ignored him.

When they came to the bottom of the staircase, Bruno pushed open the door and shoved the candle into Humbert's hands.

"Here," he said. "See for yourself."

Still smirking, Humbert wandered over to the

wall of photographs. He began to sneer at the old-fashioned haircuts and clothes. "What a bunch of losers," he pronounced, looking at a photo taken – judging by the bouffant hairdos – sometime in the nineteen-eighties. Then his mouth fell open. His head swivelled about on his neck as he looked from one photograph to another. He let out a bloodcurdling scream. The candle dropped from his hand. The chamber was plunged into darkness.

"You were right," wailed Humbert, "we *are* in terrible danger!"

"We are *now*." Bruno sighed. "How am I going to find the elixir in the dark?"

Humbert the bully had turned as wet as a football field in winter. For some reason his weakness seemed to give Bruno strength. The darkness made it harder to find the elixir, but at least it meant he didn't have to look at the photographs.

His arms stretched out like a zombie, Bruno began to feel his way around the chamber, imagining he had eyeballs in the palms of his hands. Here was the circle of golden chairs. Here was the tallest chair, where the duke had sat yesterday. The elixir must be around here somewhere…

Bruno felt along the wall behind the duke's chair

until his hands made out the contours of a small wooden cupboard. Finding the handle, he tugged open the door. At first his fingers clutched at nothing but air. Then they closed on a small glass vial… The explosive elixir! Bruno was sure of it!

While Humbert snivelled in the corner, Bruno reached into his pockets for the plastic bottles. It was easy enough to tell by their weight which one was empty and which one was full. Careful not to spill a drop, Bruno decanted the elixir into his empty plastic bottle. To think what just a few drops of this lethal liquid could do! Then, just as carefully, he refilled the glass vial with harmless water.

"Come on," he said to Humbert. "Time to see what's cooking in the kitchen."

32

Down in the Dungeons

The **clank!** of the dungeon door swinging shut behind Sir Oswald echoed in the darkness. Grandpa Trevor sank to the floor of the underground cell he now found himself locked inside, narrowly avoiding impaling himself on a stalagmite. Or was it a stalactite?

"Mites crawl *up* your legs. Tights fall *down* them," offered Julian Chalk, as if reading the old man's mind. "That's how I remember it. You know, if they weren't being used as a prison, these caves would make quite a tourist attraction."

"Oh, please stop twittering on, dear," begged his wife. "Now is not the time to be talking about rock formations."

"Sorry," replied Mr Chalk sheepishly. "You're right. Best I just shut up."

The three of them fell back into despondent silence.

After an hour or so of this, Grandpa Trevor was startled to hear a hollow sound coming from beneath his feet. He put his ear to the ground and listened. It was a muffled scraping, as if a badger or some other clawed creature was burrowing through the stone. Soon the scraping had become a rumbling, and the small patch of ground, where Grandpa Trevor had been listening, began to ripple and bulge.

"An earthquake!" cried Mrs Chalk.

The three of them looked on in alarm as part of the cave floor suddenly gave way. A mass of rock and earth disappeared into a hole that was growing wider before their eyes. Then, from out of this hole appeared first the head, then the shoulders, then the body of a man.

"Aarghhhhh!" cried Mr and Mrs Chalk together.

The man's unkempt hair stuck up in all directions. His skin was caked in mud and dust. In fact, all you could see of his face were his eyebrows, which were black and furry. One was a good deal bushier than the other. He pushed a dirty hand through his hair, revealing a pair of sticky-out ears.

Grandpa Trevor stared at the man as if he was a phantom. I must be hallucinating, he thought. "Ronald?" he said in a weak voice. "Ronald, is that really you?"

"Dad!" gasped the man, hauling himself up into the cave. "*Dad?* What are *you* doing here?"

The Chalks looked back and forth between the two men in amazement. Despite the mud and dust, the resemblance was striking. Ronald Pockley dropped to his knees and bellowed into the hole.

"Love! Get yourself up here! There's something I need to show you!" A brief delay. Then an echoing reply.

"What's the point? How many times do I have to tell you? You're tunnelling in the wrong direction..."

"Trust me. There's something I really think you should see."

A few moments later, the scruffy-looking man was joined in the cave by a dishevelled young woman.

Grandpa Trevor stared
in disbelief. Her curly hair now fell
all the way down her back and she was skinnier
than when Grandpa Trevor had last seen her. Still,
there was no mistaking his daughter-in-law Jane.

"Trevor!" she shrieked, throwing her arms
around him in joy. "But where's Bruno? Tell me!
How is he?"

Grandpa Trevor could not answer. Mrs Chalk
came forward and took the other woman's hand
in hers.

"I'm Penny Chalk. My daughter Grace is at
school with your boy Bruno. I'm afraid we have
some upsetting news."

As gently as she could, Mrs Chalk explained that Bruno and Grace had gone missing on a school trip. She told how they'd been kidnapped and brought here to Phartesia by a dastardly organization known as the Knights Trumplar. Ronald and Jane Pockley listened to this story with mounting concern.

"But what I still don't understand is what you two are doing here," said Grandpa Trevor when Mrs Chalk had finished. "I thought you were dead!"

Now it was Ronald Pockley's turn to explain. It seemed that after they'd been whipped off the roof of the block of flats, Mrs Pockley's amazing skirt balloon had carried them all the way across the Channel. Above Calais they had run into a thermal that had whisked them up and over the French Alps, eventually depositing them on a hillside in Phartesia. They'd spent a week frantically searching for a way out of the forest before Sir Oswald had found them and had them thrown in the dungeons for trespassing. Ronald had been trying to tunnel his way out ever since.

As you can imagine, Grandpa Trevor and the Chalks thought this story a little far-fetched. But then Julian Chalk remembered a documentary he'd seen on the Discovery Channel about mini-tornadoes, and declared that it was after all entirely possible.

When the tears eventually stopped falling, and it had really sunk in that at least three of the Pockleys had found each other again, it was time to decide what to do next. At first they considered waiting until Agent Frogmarch arrived with reinforcements. But they decided that the children's rescue could not be delayed any longer. With five of them all there together, they might just have a chance of overpowering the guards who were due to come with food the next day. It wasn't a very good plan, but it was the only one they had.

33
Trouble in the Kitchens

"Right," said Bruno when he and Humbert arrived back on the landing outside the dormitory. "You'll need to lead from here. You do remember the way to the kitchens, don't you?"

Humbert's thin lips quivered. "I'm n-n-not sure," he sniffed. "It'll be hard to find the w-w-way without a candle."

"Oh, for goodness' sake," said Bruno. He darted off down the corridor to borrow another candle from an alcove. "Whatever you do, don't drop this one," he warned as he returned. "Now, let's get a move on. The others will be wondering what's taking us so long."

Humbert took Bruno down the staircase that led to the dining room. Once again, Bruno was amazed at how even familiar places could become frightening in the dark. The portraits seemed to glare out of the shadows and the floorboards creaked ominously beneath their feet. Before they reached the dining hall, Humbert took a turn to the right and pushed back a heavy steel door to reveal an industrial-sized kitchen. Over in the corner stood an enormous fridge. Humbert used the candle to guide them across to it. He tugged on the fridge door and blue light spilled out into the kitchen.

It seemed that the castle chefs had been hard at work. The fridge was heaving with delicious-looking food: grilled prawns, little strawberry tarts, cheese puffs,

miniature Yorkshire puddings, frogs' legs and
sticky sausages on skewers.

Bruno wasted no time in setting to work with
the elixir. There was just enough liquid in the water
bottle to pour a tiny drop onto every canapé. It
was a much lower dosage than had been given to
Monsieur Zidler, and Bruno hoped fervently that it
would be enough.

"Right," he said, sprinkling out the last drop.
"Back to the dormitory."

Humbert suddenly clutched at Bruno's arm.
"Someone's coming!"

Before they could think of a place to hide, a
Trumpenhund bounded into the room, running
so fast that its enormous paws skidded on the
polished flagstone tiles. Sir Oswald was hot on its
heels. The children cowered behind the open fridge
door.

"Aha!" roared the knight. "What have we here,
then? Two little mice come to steal crumbs from
the kitchen?"

Bruno's brain was racing as fast as his heart.
How could they explain what they were doing out
of bed? Humbert was no use. He was just standing
there twiddling the ring on his little finger. Then,

to Bruno's surprise, his classmate found his voice.

"I'm so sorry, sir," said Humbert. "I know we're not meant to be out of bed. But we were only looking for some Stunkenstew. You see, I've been having a few problems with my phartling. I thought an extra portion might help. Bruno said he'd come with me because I'm afraid of the dark.

Sir Oswald looked stern. "By rights, I should have you both thrown into the dungeon." He chuckled to himself. "But it's getting rather crowded down there! Since you were only keen to put in a good performance, just this once I shall overlook it. Now, back to the dormitory before I change my mind!"

The two boys needed no further encouragement. They ran back to their room as fast as their legs would carry them.

"That was amazing," panted Bruno. "How did you think up a lie on the spot like that?"

"Just practice." Humbert shrugged. Although as you know, there was more truth in his lie than he cared to admit.

34
The Duke's Guest of Honour

The day of the gala concert had arrived.

An hour earlier, under the watchful eyes of the knights, the children had eaten their last bowl of Stunkenstew. They were pretty sure it wasn't poisoned, but they still found it hard to swallow. In vain, Bruno searched the serving knights' faces for some small sign of guilt or second thoughts. Instead he read there nothing but excitement. As they ate, the children heard the sound of helicopters whirring overhead.

"Aha!" pronounced Sir Oswald. "Here come our celebrity guests!"

After lunch the children were sent to polish their phartlehorns and change into freshly laundered suits. Then they joined the glamorous throng hobnobbing in the courtyard of the Chateau Mistral. The mosaics on the walls flared gold in the late afternoon sun. Rose petals had been scattered across the ground. Bunting hung from the castle turrets. The children hovered together in an anxious circle. The guests were beautiful, but there was something ghoulish about them, too. They looked dead behind the eyes, as if they had witnessed things too horrible to imagine.

Bruno looked nervously around. Where were the waiters with the canapés?

"Oh my goodness!" whispered Grace. "Look who's over there!" Bruno followed her finger. He started in shock. Dressed in a sheaf of crimson silk was a woman he'd last seen not four days before.

"It's Desiree Draws," murmured Xanadu.

It was, and it seemed the American actress had eyes for no one but the duke. She was hanging off his arm and onto his every word. The duke was dressed for the occasion in flowing pink robes. For once he had dispensed with his trusty moustache-bearers. Instead, the ends of the Royal Moustache were attached to the cuffs of his shirt with pink satin bows.

"I can't believe that someone like *her* would be in on this," said Natasha. "She looks so wholesome. That dress is from Chanel, you know."

Grace pulled a face. "My mum always says that famous people get up to some strange things. Now I understand what she means. What's wrong with normal hobbies like gardening or bird-watching?"

The duke noticed the children staring. He beckoned them over. Reluctantly, they crossed the courtyard to greet him.

"I see you've spotted this year's guest of honour," he said with a wink. "Now, don't be shy.

This is Ms Draws' f-f-first time in Phartesia and she was just telling me how she'd love to meet the children before the concert." He gave a peculiar giggle. "I'm afraid you won't have much of a chance to talk to her afterwards."

"Let's hope not," Grace muttered to herself.

The duke pushed Bruno forward. "Allow me to present our f-f-formidable solo phartiste. A young man of quite f-f-ferocious talent!"

The actress beamed down at Bruno. Her eyelashes twitched like spiders' legs as she spoke in her slow Southern drawl. "Now, isn't he the cutest thing? Won't you just look at his bushy eyebrows and sticky-out ears? Why, Dukey, if you hadn't discovered him first, I'd snap him up for a part in my next movie!" She turned to Grace. "And what's your role, sweetheart?"

Grace opened her mouth to speak, but nothing came out. The duke spoke for her.

"Miss Chalk will phartle the lead canon in Tchaikovsky's 1812 Overture. Xanadu and Natasha here will accompany." He did not mention Humbert, but for once the bully was happy to go unnoticed. He cowered behind the others, not speaking.

Desiree Draws squealed with delight. "Canons? Why, Dukey, that's inspired! Well, now I think that's going to be my favourite part."

"Oh, really?" Xanadu's smile was as fake as the starlet's nails. "I'd never have guessed."

Bruno glanced around the courtyard and breathed a sigh of relief. Waiters were weaving in and out, refilling the guests' glasses and handing round trays of poisoned canapés. As fast as the waiters could bring them out, the guests gobbled them down. Bruno prayed that the dosage would be strong enough to work. The effect on Monsieur Zidler had been almost instant. But he'd swallowed a whole bottle of the elixir. What if the guests failed to explode before the end of the concert? They'd travelled a long way to get their warped musical kicks. If they didn't, who could predict what the duke would do to save face?

Over by the entrance to the West Tower, Bruno could see the Countess Strudel flirting with a famous Latin American pop star. Was it Bruno's imagination, or had he once read some strange rumours about this man? Something about a dead body and a champagne-filled jacuzzi?

As the countess raised a poisoned vol-au-vent to

her rosebud lips, Bruno felt a pang of guilt. Then he remembered her face in the photographs. How she'd danced a little jig of joy as the exploding children sailed through the air. Bruno felt Grace nudge him gently in the ribs. He looked up to see a waiter approaching with a tray.

"Care to try a canapé, Ms Draws?" asked the duke, proffering a miniature strawberry tart.

"Well now, Dukey, you know I couldn't. As we say in Texas, a moment on the lips costs a fortune at the surgeon's." She flung back her head and let out a peel of laughter. Then, parting her scarlet lips into a honeyed smile, she bent down to Bruno. "How's about you eat mine for me, cutie?"

All five children blanched. This wasn't part of the plan.

"No, thanks," gulped Bruno. "I'm, er, feeling a bit queasy. Stage fright."

"Ah, well, that's all right, sweetie. I'll just find a waiter to take it away."

The duke snatched the canapé from Ms Draws. He crouched down beside Bruno. "Didn't your mother ever teach you that it's bad manners to refuse a gift?"

Suddenly, the duke's smile had turned into a

snarl. He pushed the canapé towards Bruno's face. "Eat it!" he ordered.

Bruno shook his head. "Sorry," he said through closed lips, "but I'm really not hungry."

"Honestly, Dukey," begged Ms Draws, "don't make the boy eat it if he doesn't want to."

But the duke was not to be denied his sport. Helpless, the other children watched as he squeezed Bruno's cheeks between his jewelled white fingers. Bruno's lips opened into a squashed ellipse. The duke forced in the canapé.

"There now," he said, holding his hand over Bruno's face long enough for to him swallow. "Don't tell me that wasn't f-f-fabulous."

Bruno couldn't speak.

Desiree Draws dragged on the duke's arm to steer him away from the children. Just then, Sir Oswald appeared and stopped the duke in his tracks. "Your Majesty. May I have a word with you in private?"

"What is it?" demanded the duke. "Can't you see I've got company?"

Sir Oswald nodded at Desiree Draws. "I'm sorry to interrupt, ma'am. But I really do think, Your Majesty, that it would be better if we talked in private."

The starlet pouted, flicking back her golden waves of hair. "Come now, soldier, you're not going to take my Dukey away from me, are you? Not when I've flown all this way just to see him. Why, I'm sure there's nothing you can't say in front of a harmless gal like me and these five innocent little children. You're not keeping secrets from me, are you, Dukey?"

The duke had turned as pink as a sugared almond. "You know I could never keep secrets f-f-from you, Ms Draws. What is it you want to tell me, Sir Oswald?"

The Phartesian Chief of Security stood to attention. "Very well," he said. "I am afraid the prisoners we caught last night are causing something of a disturbance. They have been attempting to fight their way out of the dungeon. One of my guards has sustained a rather painful injury in a rather personal place."

"Well then, what are you standing here f-f-for?" barked the duke. "Get rid of them! And since we have guests, I trust I can rely on you to deal with the matter discreetly?"

Sir Oswald nodded and turned to walk away. "Stop!" cried Desiree Draws. *"Deal with them*

264

discreetly? Why now, Dukey, don't you dare! A man as powerful as you should never do anything *discreetly*. Do things discreetly and folks might get the impression you care what they think. A powerful man like you should deal with anyone who disobeys you right out in the open."

The duke clapped his jewelled hands in glee. "What a splendid idea!" he squealed. "Now come along, Ms Draws, I must introduce you to my daughter."

Hand in hand, they walked off across the courtyard to where Strudel was still fawning over the pop star.

"Quick!" whispered Grace as soon as they were out of earshot. "Spit it out!"

Xanadu clapped Bruno on the back as he coughed the soggy strawberry tart up into his hand.

"I tried not to swallow any," he gasped. "But it's hard to be sure. What if I've eaten enough for the elixir to work on me?"

Natasha looked nervous. "Don't be silly," she said, struggling to sound like her normal cynical self. "That tart looks as good as new to me. I'm sure there's not a single crumb missing."

Bruno stared down at the pink and beige mush in his hand. "Thanks for trying. But we all know that's a lie." He paused. "The thing is, the tart's not the only thing worrying me. What if the guests don't start exploding before the end of the concert? There's no way they'll leave Phartesia without witnessing the destruction they've come to see. All the knights would have to do would be to give us another dose of the elixir."

Grace's face was determined. "Bruno," she said. "I think it's time to resort to Plan C."

"There's a Plan C? Brilliant! What is it?"

"Stay calm and keep our fingers crossed."

35

This Year's Solo Phartiste!

"Thirty seconds to go!" called a stagehand.

Darkness engulfed the Phartling Hall, where everyone was now gathered, ready for the concert to begin. At the flick of a switch a single spotlight illuminated the Royal Box. The audience fell silent.

Into the golden circle of light flounced the duke. He lifted his hands, unfurling the twin strands of his moustache like a pair of silver wings.

"My dear f-f-friends," he declared, "it gives me great pleasure to welcome you to our annual Grand Gala Concert! As always, I can promise you an evening of truly explosive entertainment!"

The audience guffawed with laughter.

267

Bruno stood behind the velvet curtains, prickling with rage. Now that he finally understood the duke's jokes, he knew how deadly serious they were. He glanced over at Grace. She was staring nervously down at her fingers, all of which were crossed. Behind her, as if for protection, Xanadu, Humbert and Natasha clutched their phartlehorns tightly to their chests.

"In keeping with the glorious traditions of Phartesia," continued the duke, "the concert will begin with the f-f-famous aria from *The Magic Phartlehorn*. So, without f-f-further ado, if you could please join me in giving a warm welcome to this year's solo phartiste, Bruno Pockley!"

As the curtains rolled back, the applause from the audience was deafening. Now the spotlight shone directly on Bruno. He squinted out into the sea of faces. It was hard to make out much, but sitting in the front row he could just about recognize the beautiful Desiree Draws.

The duke flicked down with his baton and the countess struck up the first tune on the piano.

There was nothing Bruno could do but play. His fingers fumbled for their place on the keys. He took a deep breath and blasted out through his phartlehorn: **Parp, parp, parpagena**.

The audience gasped. Never before had they heard such a talent!

Despite everything, Bruno felt a sudden surge of pride. Instinctively he knew that he could control the emotions of every single person in the room in the way that the moon controls the sea. For five blissful minutes he abandoned himself to the music. The walls of the Phartling Hall echoed with the sound of breaking wind. Bruno's worries floated away on the ebbs and flows of his own exquisite expulsions.

Then it was over. There was a moment's silence before the audience erupted. They jumped to their feet. They whooped and hollered and whistled and cheered. Tears formed in Bruno's eyes. This was all he had ever wanted. To phartle in front of an audience. To have his talent appreciated. If only Grandpa Trevor and his parents had been there to hear him play.

But Grandpa Trevor was far away, back on *The Jolly Codger* with Chippy.

And his parents were dead and gone.

36

The Grand Finale

The countess had moved on to the next tune. Bruno halfheartedly joined in. Already he could sense the adrenalin trickling out through his toes. Never again would he know such happiness.

Now that Bruno's moment in the sun was over, he felt his fears mount up like overdue homework. Even now a poisoned crumb from the strawberry tart could be whizzing its way around his intestines, casting spells upon his cells and preparing to send him hurtling into the air. And why oh why had no one in the audience started to explode?

"Air on the G String" passed without incident. As the orchestra performed the opening interlude of Wagner's Ring Cycle, Bruno scanned the sea of faces in a vain attempt to spot a trace of discomfort. But everyone he could see looked bright-eyed and rosy-cheeked.

He glanced across at Grace. Her face was white with terror as she waited to play. Bruno could guess what she was thinking: they should have tried to escape while they still had the chance.

"There's no way out now," she whispered, catching his eye. "The doors to the Phartling Hall are locked. If people don't start exploding soon, we're finished!"

All too soon, the first movement of Wagner's Ring Cycle had come to an end. Next on the bill was the 1812 Overture: the piece in which the children would phartle the part of the canons; the piece in which they were due to go up in smoke.

Bruno felt a strange fizzing in his stomach. He prayed that it was just fear, and not the elixir starting to take effect.

The duke turned to face the audience. "Dearest f-f-friends," he declared, "I trust that you have enjoyed our concert so f-f-far. Now we come to the part f-f-for which I know you have all been waiting. I am delighted to announce an unexpected addition to tonight's programme. Some political prisoners have been attempting to escape from my dungeons. I was going to deal with them in private, but our guest of honour, Ms Desiree Draws, has suggested that you might all like to witness the spectacle of their deaths!"

The audience roared their approval.

"What's going on?" whispered Natasha. "What's he talking about? Why haven't the audience started to explode? I *told* you we should have made a run for it!"

Grace looked down at the floor.

"If we'd done that, we'd have been caught for certain," said Bruno, rushing to her defence.

Sir Oswald marched the prisoners out onto the stage. Bruno's breath caught in his throat. They were huddled together so tightly that it was hard to make out all their faces. But three of them looked just like Grandpa Trevor and his parents! His stomach lurched with nausea. The poisoned canapé must be playing tricks on his mind.

Grace stumbled forwards as if she was about to faint. "Mum! Dad!" she managed to gasp.

Bruno looked on in bewildered horror as the prisoners were ordered to kneel. The audience was on its feet now, jeering and baying for blood.

"*Noooo!*" screamed Bruno, coming to his senses.

"Stop! Please stop!"

But it was too late. Sir Oswald was already standing over Grandpa Trevor and drawing his sword. There was nothing Bruno could do. A phalanx of knights barred his way.

Then Bruno saw a woman in red jump up from the front row and dart across the stage. Whipping off a red-soled stiletto, she flung it like a spear towards Sir Oswald's head. He let out a screech of pain as the heel spiked him in the back of his skull.

"Take zat, you brute!" she yelled in a strong French accent.

Gobsmacked, Bruno watched as the woman scissor-kicked the sword from the knight's hand. Snatching it up from the ground, she bravely fought back the other knights who were now rushing towards her. It was Desiree Draws! But why did she sound French? And why was she trying to save them?

"Don't just stand there," she shouted at the children and the prisoners. "Fight for your lives!"

The children snapped out of their trance. Dressed in their black-and-white suits, they looked like a battalion of penguins. But penguins don't have weapons at their disposal – and the children did. Metal clanged against metal as they fended off the knights' swords with their phartlehorns. The duke jumped down from the Royal Box, drew out his sword and charged at Desiree Draws. A furious duel broke out between them. Meanwhile, the other guests, anxious to escape the scene of the crime, were scrabbling out of their seats and running for the door.

Bruno thwacked away a knight, then glanced back across the stage. Humbert, Xanadu, Natasha and Grace were all doing their bit. Mrs Chalk was duelling with the countess. Grandpa Trevor was using a candelabra to batter Sir Oswald. Mr Chalk was thumping Jobsworth with his thermos flask. Was that *really* his mum and dad Bruno could see fighting valiantly with a pair of music stands?

The duke broke free from Desiree Draws and tried to make a run for it across the stage. Bruno stuck out his foot and he stumbled to the floor.

"Good work, cutie!" shouted Desiree Draws.

Bruno gave her a grin.

Too late, he turned to see the duke staggering back to his feet clutching a heavy wooden clog. Time seemed to pass in slow motion as the duke raised the clog in the air. Bruno's heart somersaulted in his chest. Was it his imagination or was there smoke billowing from the duke's ears?

There was!

Suddenly, the duke dropped the clog and clutched his hands to his stomach. His skin turned a deep purple and his eyes began to bulge in his face. His throat was making a strange rattling sound. More smoke streamed from his ears as he ran round and round in little circles. Then, as if someone had released the end of a balloon, the duke whizzed up into the air and did a loop-the-loop around the ceiling, letting off a long, squelching raspberry of a phartle.

Hypnotized, Bruno's eyes followed the duke's journey through the air. As he flew up to greet the painted cherubs, his moustache snagged around a branch of the chandelier. For a few seconds he hung there, legs kicking wildly. Then, **KABOOM! KAPOOF!** The duke was nothing but a shower of silvery ash raining down upon the stage.

"We did it!" cried Bruno, shaking the soot from his hair and running towards Grandpa Trevor and his parents. "We're sav—"

But before he could finish, Bruno felt the fizzing feeling in his stomach again. There was no mistaking it this time. It was as if he had swallowed a box of washing powder and it was bubbling away in his guts. Bruno thought he heard his mother calling his name across the theatre. Then his whole world went black.

Too late for him to see, Agent Frogmarch and a hundred British troops came crashing through the doors.

Reaping the Rewards

Two days later, when Bruno next opened his eyes, he found himself staring straight up into the face of an angel. An angel who looked remarkably like the film star Desiree Draws.

"He's awake!" exclaimed Grandpa Trevor, pushing the angel out of the way and planting a big wet kiss on his grandson's cheek.

"Oh, Bruno, you're alive!" cried Grace, rushing over to his bedside.

Bruno looked around the white room filled with white furniture and bleeping white machines. "What happened?" he asked, looking from Grace to Grandpa Trevor to the angel in amazement. "Am I in heaven?"

"'Fraid not," chuckled his grandpa. "This is a top

London hospital. The doc says you're to stay in bed for observation, but they don't think there'll be any lasting damage."

Slowly, the clouds in Bruno's memory began to clear. "I don't understand," he said, goggling at Desiree Draws. "You were there at the concert … but then you rescued us."

A stout, ferocious-looking woman with bobbed helmet-hair jumped up from a chair in the corner. She snorted in disgust.

"Double Agent Draws and the French intelligence service may try to take the glory, but your rescue came courtesy of Her Majesty the Queen of England! I am Agent Frogmarch and I saved you … along with a crack team of SAS troops."

"Double Agent Draws? French intelligence service?" repeated Bruno, mystified. "But I thought you were a famous Hollywood actress."

"Well now, cutie," drawled Double Agent Draws before reverting back to her natural French accent, "movies are just something zat I do on the side. Every spy needs a cover. I find that acting and espionage go together like champagne and frogs' legs. Though while we're in the business of handing out credit, it was actually you and Grace here who saved the day by swapping those potions. Oh, and we mustn't forget your Grandpa Trevor, who parachuted in to find you."

Bruno looked up at Grandpa Trevor in awe. "You jumped out of a plane?"

His grandfather grinned his tobacco-stained grin. "Chippy came too, disguised as an owl."

"Twit-twoo," squawked Chippy. "Twit-twoo!"

Bruno laughed until his ribs hurt. "What about the others?" he asked. "Natasha, Xanadu and Humbert? They're all OK, aren't they?"

"They're all fine," Grace reassured him.

Desiree Draws smiled. "As a very close friend of mine likes to say, they're shaken but not stirred."

Bruno giggled. It was strange, but he was even glad Humbert was all right. The days in the castle had brought everyone closer together.

"What about the knights?" he asked. "The duke and his daughter?"

"All gone up in smoke," replied Agent Frogmarch, brushing imaginary dust from her hands. "Thanks to you, phartistry is finally a thing of the past. There's not a single person left on the planet who'd pay to hear you phartle!"

Bruno knew he should be pleased, but instead his heart sank. He'd found the one thing in life he was really good at and now he'd never be able to do it again. Then an image of the prisoners standing onstage in the Phartling Hall came to him through a fog of memory. He turned to his grandfather.

"I thought I saw Mum and Dad with you there in Phartesia. The elixir must have made me imagine things."

Grandpa Trevor blinked back another rush of tears. He glanced up at Agent Frogmarch. She gave a curt nod. The old man struggled to pull himself together. "The doctors asked us not to tell you... Said the shock would be too much... But, well, it doesn't seem right to keep it from you..."

Agent Frogmarch was looking impatient. "You can come in now," she barked.

Two familiar figures appeared in the doorway. Over a year had passed since the day they floated out of his life, and Bruno couldn't believe that at last they were here again.

"Mum! Dad!" he cried.

Overwhelmed by emotion, his parents ran to his bedside. "Oh son, I was so proud of you," sobbed his mother, squeezing him tight. "Your phartling was incredible!"

"You heard me play the solo in *The Magic Phartlehorn*?" asked Bruno, incredulous.

"Of course we did," said his dad. "We were waiting tied up in the wings. And if those knights had killed me, I'd have died a happy man."

"Hallelujah!" squawked Chippy. "Hallelujah!"

Bruno could hardly take it all in. Never had he felt such happiness. Who cared about becoming famous? He had his family back together again!

Just as Mrs Pockley began to explain how they'd come to be in Phartesia in the first place, there came the sound of a scuffle outside in the corridor. Bruno felt a stab of pain in his ribs as he coughed. He could have sworn there was a whiff of smoke in the air.

"I don't give a toasted turnip that you're the nurse in charge," shouted an angry voice, "I demand to see the boy this instant!"

"I'm afraid I can't let you in, Mr Oblonksy. Visiting at this time is strictly for friends and family."

Natasha's father burst into the room. His foul-smelling cigar stuck out of his face like a factory chimney as he barged his way over to Bruno's bed. "So this is the little squirt, is it?" he puffed. "Why, if it wasn't for him, my beautiful daughter would be—"

"Nothing but a putrid pile of ash," finished Desiree Draws, plucking the cigar from his mouth and grinding it under her heel. "Which, my darling, is exactly what you'll be if you keep on smoking these revolting things. There, look how much more handsome you are without it."

The tips of Mr Oblonksy's ears had turned bright red. "You could at least have let me finish my *sentence*," he grumbled. "Natasha told me everything that went on in that castle. I promised a reward to anyone who could bring her home to me in one piece."

Mr Oblonsky reached into his pocket. He pulled out his cheque book and a fountain pen made from solid gold. "From what my daughter tells me, it's Bruno and Grace who deserve that reward. I've

282

come here to give it to them. Here's one for you, Miss Chalk," he said, signing his name with a flourish. "And here's one for you, Mr Pockley."

Bruno's eyes widened. Never had he seen so many noughts. He counted them on his fingers.

"*Charity begins at home*," squawked Chippy, pecking at the cheque. "*Charity begins at home*."

Bruno laughed. "Don't worry, Chippy," he said. "From now on you'll only eat the finest organic mango."

Agent Frogmarch escorted Mr Oblonsky from the room. Double Agent Draws turned to the children with a smile. "And as a small token of gratitude from French intelligence…"

She handed Grace a small white envelope. Grace tore it open and pulled out a photograph of a black-and-white puppy. Written on the back was: *Buster – who can't wait to meet his new owner, Grace!*

Grace gasped. "But how did you know that's what I've always wanted?"

"We're spies, Miss Chalk," said Desiree Draws,

and winked. "It's our job to know what a person most desires."

"A skill I hope you'll learn from us someday," announced Agent Frogmarch, stomping back into the room. "For in recognition of your impressive strategic planning in the face of danger, Her Majesty's Secret Service would like to offer you a spot of work experience."

"Wow!" exclaimed Grace. "That'd be awesome."

Meanwhile Desiree Draws had disappeared out into the corridor. She returned with a box, wrapped in brown paper, about the size of a small chest of drawers.

"This one's for you, Bruno," she said with a smile.

Chippy helped Bruno to pull back the wrapping. Inside was a cracked leather case. Bruno tried the lid, but it was locked.

"You'll need this," said Desiree Draws and handed him a small golden key. Bruno turned it over in his palm. The fob was sculpted into the shape of a man with a long handlebar moustache. The ancient symbol of the Knights Trumplar!

Nervously, he turned the key in the lock. The faintest clicking sound. Then the lid sprang back.

284

Bruno blinked. Nestling inside the case was the most beautiful instrument he had ever seen. It was a phartlehorn – but not like any of the phartlehorns Bruno had seen in Phartesia. The one he had played at the castle was hammered from brass. This was hewn from sparkling gold and set with rubies and emeralds. The body of a dragon was engraved around the tube.

"A gift to Monsieur John Pujol from the Emperor of China," explained Desiree Draws. "We confiscated it from the duke's treasury. I think Pujol would have wanted you to have it."

"Who's John Pujol?" asked Mrs Pockley.

"John Pujol was the greatest phartiste ever to have lived," explained Bruno.

"Apart from you, of course!" cut in Grandpa Trevor. He turned to Agent Frogmarch. "I thought you said phartistry was banned?"

"It is, Mr Pockley," she assured him. "But we're spies. Sometimes it's our job to see everything. Sometimes it's our job to turn a blind eye."

"You mean I'm allowed to play it in public?" asked Bruno.

"Not in the playground," warned Agent Frogmarch. "But I'm sure a few private concerts could be overlooked. Her Majesty's Secret Service believes that every child has a talent. Where would this great country be if we stood by and let those talents go to waste?"

Bruno watched, speechless, as Agent Frogmarch picked up the phartlehorn and wrestled it down over her stout frame.

"Always wanted to try one of these things," she muttered. "Purely for research purposes, of course. Tell me, how does it work?" The special agent struggled to squeeze out a phartle.

"That's the way to do it!" squawked Chippy. "That's the way to do it!"

Acknowledgements

Anyone can tell a story, but it takes lots of people working together to make a book, and I would like to thank all of the people who have helped in the creation of this one.

First of all, huge thanks to my agent, Jo Unwin, for plucking me from the slush pile to be her first ever client and for all the support she and the rest of the team at Conville & Walsh have given me along the way. Thanks also to Jane Winterbotham, Jacky Paynter, Rebecca Harper and all at Walker Books, and especially to my editor, Emma Lidbury: without her beady eye, everything in this book would be silver and happen at midnight.

No author could hope for a better illustrator than Hannah Shaw: she might be allergic to musical instruments but she sure draws a mean phartlehorn. Special thanks are also owed to Mouse Matthews for loaning me Bruno's surname, which is of her own invention; and to Grace, Jules and Penny Chalkey for lending me their real(ish) names if not their characters. I must also thank Jules and his creative partner, Nick Simons, plus my very own Great Producer, Keeley Pratt, for their help with the launch marketing campaign. Thanks are also due to my old friend Eliot Wykes, with whom the idea of a very different story about musical farting was first discussed. For his professional expertise and moral support, I owe a debt of gratitude to David Allen Green; as I do to the Arvon Foundation: my determination to complete a children's book was fortified by a week of scribbling, daydreaming and dancing on the tables at their centre in Moniack Mhor, an experience I will never forget.

Before I could read, my parents read to me: the greatest gift you could ever give a child. Nor must I forget my sister, Beth, whose friendship has been invaluable to me whilst writing this book. Finally, the biggest thanks of all must go to Kit, who gave me the best gifts I could have wanted as an adult: time to write, and love, and, most crucially of all, who invented the rare breed Trumpenhund.